BODY IN THE SURGERY

A RITA PATEL MYSTERY

By Catherine Cooper

Oxford eBooks

Chapter

1

"Anybody who enjoys being in the House of Commons probably needs psychiatric help."

Ken Livingstone

Sunday, 20th October 2013 11am

I watch you every day. As the Police (there's an irony) song goes "Every Step You Take, Every Move You Make." I watch you on TV - you make it so easy for me with your appearances on politics shows, Question Time, Newsnight. You're quite a publicity whore aren't you? You are due on Sunday Politics today. When you're not on my screens I follow you on Twitter and Facebook, and I read your blog, or I just follow you. I know where you live (both your houses, and I know you fiddle your expenses) and I know where you work. I know your diary before you do (the power of hacking) and, unlike you, I check it regularly. So I know when you're in the House, when you're in Committee, when you are at Parliamentary meetings and when you're seeing constituents or your local party activists.

I know when you're in Leicester (not often enough really is it? Considering you're a local MP) and when you're in London (which is where you prefer to be, wining and dining in SW1, networking and working your way up the greasy power pole). I probably know, although I prefer not to think about it, when you eat and shit and shag and sleep. I should make a blog about that. Would anyone read it though? You're so predictable and easy to follow that watching you does not exactly take up all my time. Which is good, because then I have time for other work, the jobs I take to provide the services you need. Yes, sometimes I am watching you from very close indeed. But you, you don't really see me, do you? People like you don't waste time on the little people, not unless you have a use for us of course.

And what if you do? You use us and throw us away when you're done. It's on to the next. But you don't tell Andrew Neil or Andrew Marr about that do you? That part of your life, the secret part that stays hidden. Well, all that is about to change, my friend.

I followed you down into the Underground and watched you get off at Westminster station. There is a special entrance to the Houses of Parliament from the Westminster tube for your kind, isn't there? For people like you with special passes. (And me, by the way, I made sure I have a pass too.) I've seen you swan through the rotating gate, neck held high, leaving Departmental officials to scurry round to the other entrance and be subjected to the humiliating security processes of being photographed and searched before they rejoin you in the carpeted corridors of power.

I stood behind you on the Jubilee line platform at Baker Street; with the prod of one finger, well maybe two, you are rather overweight, I could have sent you spilling under the train. But then you wouldn't have known why you were dying, so that wouldn't do. I want to whisper in your ear so you know when the end has come.

* * *

Monday, 21st October 2013 5pm

The people you like to have around you are very young – 19 or 20 – there's a reason for that isn't there? Young and keen and not worldly wise, wanting to impress and get on and not wanting to upset people in authority, people like you. That's how you get away with it, until now.

I followed you 'round the garden centre the other day. You didn't see me. Too busy playing the big man with your family, pulling faces at babies in buggies and patting constituents' children on the head. What a warm glow all that recognition must have given you. Well I recognise you. I recognise you for what you are. They would not look so adoringly at you if they knew what I know; if they'd seen what I've seen.

There you were, thumbing through the pot plants, the heathers and the cacti. Mind you don't prick your fingers! I'd hate you to hurt yourself. Admiring the goldfish and stroking the rabbits in pets' corner, bestowing your benevolence on hamsters and guinea pigs in their cages. What a nice man! Kind to children and animals! Hypocrite!

I saw you in the gift section. Were you seriously going to buy those boots? I did not have you down as the outdoor type. The kitchen equipment seemed to be more your kind of thing, coffee pots and fondu sets, mugs with every letter of the alphabet. You chatted to your family – I assume that's who that motley collection of people were – a fatter version of you in cheaper clothes, was that your brother perhaps? There were two women – your wife and his? Or was it a sister, perhaps? I really should look up your family history, although you've done your best to hide it, haven't you? Are you ashamed of something? But then, you've plenty to be ashamed about.

The child in the wheelchair was the only one I felt sorry for. He was coughing constantly - cystic fibrosis maybe? The one where the parents have to clear out the lungs? The child was constantly playing on a computer game which sang tunes like advert jingles every five minutes or so and the child talked in a high pitched breathless way, as I suppose you would, if your lungs were filling up with fluid all the time. Hard to say how old he was. Not yours though, I guess? You just got the kudos for being seen out with him. You never pushed him, or talked to him, you left that to your brother and the women. Too much like getting your hands dirty perhaps?

I hid behind the greetings cards when you went for a drink in the café. I watched you over the rows of 'Get Well' cards as you sipped at your cup; another irony, I don't wish you well at all, as you will find out tomorrow.

* * *

Tuesday, 22nd October 2013 4pm

It is 4 o'clock in the afternoon. Rita Patel, aged 17 and living with her family at 10 Elm Drive in Leicester, has survived over 24 hours on her own ('home alone' as she likes to call it), two concerned phone calls from her parents on holiday in India ("just checking you are are all right; we got here safely; your cousins send their love") and one from her Aunt Jaina ("let me know if you need anything, your mother wants me to keep an eye on you"). Rita is having a driving lesson with Mr Patel ('no relation' as she and her brother like to joke). She plans to have several lessons in the half term holiday, so she can learn to drive as soon as possible, having lessons in the evenings is difficult because of homework and her after school activities. Rita is impatient to learn; she cannot wait until she can drive herself to school!

The red Corsa, adapted as a driving school car, has a sign on the roof proclaiming 'SUCCESS SCHOOL OF MOTORING. You can't fail with us!' When he had first seen Mr Patel's car, Jahi, Rita's father, had had his doubts, and wondered if he should put in a call to Trading Standards; but when Mr Patel got Rita's older brother, Mohal, through his driving test first time, Jahi had to admit some admiration and so is hopeful that Mr Patel can work his magic with his daughter too.

Rita is on the dual carriageway ('At last!' she thinks) on Aylestone Road. Despite her wish to go fast (expressed on the telephone to her friend, Priya Shah, who admires Rita's confidence), Rita has in reality crept up to only 27 miles per hour. Cars are queuing to get into the outside lane to pass her, but she is oblivious to this, as she concentrates on keeping the correct pressure on the accelerator and worries about changing down from the fourth gear she has finally put the vehicle into. ('This is harder than it looks,' she is thinking.)

"Check your rear-view mirror," Mr Patel reminds her, stroking at his goatee beard thoughtfully. Rita glances up. To her horror, behind her car she can see the blue flashing light of a police car.

"Oh dear." says Rita, "What do I do?"

"Well, normally in these situations," Mr Patel says slowly, "I advise pulling over to the left so the police can pass. However," he adds more quickly as Rita's hand hovers over the indicator as if over the trigger of a gun, "In this instance, it is clear to me that the police do not wish to go by you."

"No?" Rita stops breathing for a moment, it is all she can do to keep her hands on the wheel and her eyes looking at the road ahead.

"No. If they wanted to do that, they would move into the outside lane." Mr Patel explains reasonably.

"So?" Rita's vocabulary is diminishing as the car rolls along; Mr Patel notes her speed has reduced to 25 mph and is grateful that the vehicle is charitable to new drivers, as Rita has not even considered changing down the gears yet.

"So it is us they want to talk to. See, they are flashing their lights." he points out patiently.

"Oh yes." Rita braves another glance in the rear view mirror.

Mr Patel continues slowly, as if advising Rita how to dismantle an explosive device,

"So slow down gradually, indicating left, and pull into the side... that's it, 3rd gear, 2nd, 1st," he talks her down the gears. Rita hits the brake pedal and the car jerks forward a little then rocks back as she brings it to a halt.

"Well, this is a first!" says Mr Patel as his red car is bathed in the blue light of the police car which has pulled in behind them.

Rita is beginning to wish she had been more cautious. What will her parents say if she is in trouble? And she must report this to Priya, and tell her brother, Mohal. As she brings the car to rest by the kerb, Rita recalls her most recent telephone conversations with her friend and with her brother.

* * *

Monday, 21st October 2013 2pm

Rita had been on her own for 1 hour and 30 minutes before she decided to skype her best friend from school. Her parents, Padma and Jahi, had set off, with her younger brother, Nayan, for a flight to India to spend half term with relatives there. Rita left the sanctuary of her pink bedroom to go down the spiral staircase to the large, modern kitchen which was installed to the delight of her mother last year. Rita prepared nachos and cheese some of which she scooped up into her mouth with her fingers, then licked them and called Priya Shah on Skype.

"So the family have gone?" Priya's oval face and long, neat brown black hair appeared on the screen which Rita had placed on the kitchen worktop. "And how's Mohal getting on?" Priya inquired casually, although she has always had a soft spot for Rita's older brother and is anxious about his welfare. Between mouthfuls of nachos, Rita explained he was enjoying the internship at Parliament and getting familiar with all the terminology and jargon, which he insisted on explaining to her.

"Great!" said Priya, then, reaching across the screen she reappeared with a comb in her hand as she asked. "Now remind me, how did Parliament first start? Was it to do with Simon de Montfort? The one the Hall and the other

8

University are named after? Did it all start in Leicester?" Priya bombarded her friend with questions to which she knew that Rita, with her interest in history, would probably know the answer.

"Not exactly," Rita did not disappoint (she had done a module that covers this period) "A lot of people think of Simon de Montfort as holding the first Parliament but it wasn't quite like that. He did rule instead of the King for while and was the first to involve what you might call common people in the process, but it wasn't Parliament like we know it now and he was really a bit of a tyrant, actually." Rita explained.

"But he was from Leicester? Else why would there be a Uni and a concert hall with his name?" Priya interrupted, puzzled now.

"He was the Earl of Leicester, that's the association," Rita went on "But he wasn't from here, he wasn't even English!"

"What? How does that work?" Priya asked indignantly.

"Well, the King, Henry III, lost power to Simon de Montfort and a council in 1265." Rita continued, "It all started with Magna Carta, really, in 1215." On the screen Rita could see her friend putting the comb through her long dark hair, a habit of hers.

"So what's that got to do with Parliament? And where does Simon de Montfort come in?" Priya prompted.

Before Rita could answer, Priya could hear the sound of Rita's mobile ringing out – the One Direction track echoing in her friend's house.

"Sorry, got to go!" Rita had said, trying to talk and swallow nachos at the same time,

"That will be Mohal, I'd better tell him they got off safely. I'll call you after my driving lesson tomorrow!"

'Typical of Rita not to finish her explanation!' thought Priya.

"See ya." she said as she laid down her comb.

"So the parents got off okay?" Mohal Patel asked his younger sister, talking on his mobile during a break in his work. Mohal was staying with his aunt (his great aunt to be accurate) at her house in Neasden. Mohal, a second year journalism student, was living there temporarily so that he could work (for nothing) at the House of Commons for a local MP, Mervyn Halliwell, as part of his University course. As she chatted to her brother, Rita, who had moved back upstairs, checked herself in the mirror in her bedroom – patting down her curly brown hair to try to get it to look as if it belonged on her head, and worrying about whether she had spots on the smudge of a nose that emerged from her round face.

"Yeah, no dramas. Mum had it sorted. Whenever Dad said 'Have we got the tickets?' or 'Where are the passports?' she would produce them from one of the pockets in her cabin bag."

"And Nayan managed not to include any sharp objects in his luggage?" Mohal sounded sceptical.

"I hope so!" exclaimed Rita, who was dubious about the grip on reality of her scatter-brained 14 year old brother whose main preoccupation seemed to be computer games.

"Let's pray he didn't say 'bomb' at the wrong moment, like in that film 'Meet the Fokkers.'" joked Rita's older brother; two months into his internship, and isolated from his student friends, he was feeling just a little homesick, missing the banter with his siblings and his mother's home cooking, not that he would admit that to anyone.

"Yeah. All that organising. And the effort it took to get the visas! You would not think it would be so difficult. Good job Mum got it sorted on the computer with help from your friends in the Library." (Mohal worked in the Central Library in Leicester in the holidays).

"Yeah. Don't tell everyone about the Library, though, they'd have a queue out of the door; they just helped as a favour. It's important to get the paperwork right, the security people can be very fussy, especially with Asian people." Mohal asserted. (Rita thought, here we go, another of Mohal's conspiracy theories. The planes to India would be full of Asians so how could that work? But she was aware that Mohal's distrust of the police and security staff had grown since he went to University. Rita thought he felt picked on for his appearance and he was always saying that white students didn't get stopped and questioned as often as he did.)

"How's the job?" she decided to change the subject.

"Oh, I'm enjoying it." Mohal told her. "I get to see Mr Halliwell quite a lot especially at Portcullis House, we call it PCH for short." he added, explaining that Mr Halliwell and other MPs had offices in that building, and failing to admit to his sister that his role was mostly to fetch coffees and carry papers. At least he was seeing the unwritten British constitution in action.

"We get to write replies to letters from constituents. You find out about all sorts happening locally – planning permissions, library closures, the effect of HS2 on Leicester – you know the fast train line to Birmingham they want to build?" he had explained for Rita's benefit . "I've chatted to some of the political advisers and I've got to know a guy working in communications for DCLG, that's the Communities and Local Government Department, I might like to have a go at that one day."

"Sounds like you're kept busy." Rita was impressed to hear her brother so interested and animated, and with the familiarity he was showing with the terminology. This internship was doing him some good, she thought.

"Yeah, not so bad. We get lots of down-time too. Mr Halliwell's not there all the time and, after all, I'm not being paid. But I do get to work around Westminster and Portcullis House, that's where Mr Halliwell does a lot of work and meets constituents when it's not convenient to meet them in

Leicester. They call it a surgery."

Mervyn Halliwell, Rita knew, was the instantly recognisable MP for the Leicester (North) constituency. In his early forties, he had a thick thatch of unruly brown hair that never looked tidy and fell across his eyes; in addition he always sported a bow tie. There was something of the Bertie Wooster about his appearance, except that Wooster would have had an efficient Jeeves to keep his image and enthusiasm in check. Instead, Mr Halliwell engaged a team of unpaid young people, mostly men, who keenly tried to keep on top of his correspondence and liaised with his diary secretary who was a large, well-manicured, mature woman – 'lady Camilla' as he called her - who acted as a surrogate mother, a Wendy figure, to all the 'lost boys'.

Rita had seen the MP up close recently. She had been taking part in a tourism survey in Leicester city centre, asking members of the public where they had travelled from, how often they made the journey, and how much they expected to spend. Rita's group were largely girls, all dressed down, in t-shirts, tracksuit bottoms and trainers, and they had spent some time, draped gracefully like nymphs, on benches in Town Hall Square, inventing responses to the questionnaire to save time (if they only did a few no one would know, they reasoned). This gave more time for gossip and a drink from McDonalds before they needed to head back to school. On this indolent scene had alighted the MP for Leicester North, on his way to attend a meeting with local councillors about the Government's 'spare room subsidy' or 'bedroom tax' (the name depending on your point of view) – a policy to prevent housing benefit claimants from having 'spare bedrooms' - and its unforeseen consequences on the individuals concerned and the housing stock.

"Hello guys." he had greeted them, taking in the scene, the girls sitting or lying on the benches, two boys standing behind them like patriarchs in a Victorian painting.

"Good weather for a change!" he had observed; the early autumn had produced a soft warm day, as if the harsher winds of the season were as yet far off, lulling everyone into false optimism. In the flesh he was better looking than on TV, Rita had decided; television made his complexion look ruddy and flushed – maybe they put too much makeup on him. In person, she could see, he had clear, healthy skin. No one had known exactly how to respond to this interruption, but Rohan had said gruffly "Tourism survey, sir, good day to do it!" and Mr Halliwell had nodded as if tourism was the only thing he cared about at that moment, then he had moved on, with his assistants following.

Mohal was spending time with the MP as part of his journalism and media course at Hertfordshire University, having indicated an interest in political journalism ('I'd like to be a spin doctor!' he had announced to his amazed family one day. They were unaware he knew anything about politics at all). At the beginning of December, Mohal will be replaced by another student. In return for penning helpful-sounding, but vague, replies to the letters Mervyn Halliwell receives, and finding out who else might usefully be contacted on a particular matter ('Parliamentary etiquette does not permit'; 'I have referred your query to the appropriate Department' etc.), Mohal was acquiring first-hand experience of how government and party politics work. Mr Halliwell was generous with his time, seeing Mohal on several occasions each day, especially as Mohal made sure he got to the office early and left late, for which purpose he had his own office key.

Mohal even got to answer Mr Halliwell's phone sometimes as the MP moved around the winding corridors of the House of Commons and across Whitehall and back between the House and his office at Portcullis House, a modern building built in an old style opposite the Houses of Parliament. Although he does not drink alcohol himself, Mohal had been pleased to be invited, with others on the staff, to a couple of drinking sessions with Mr Halliwell after late night debates and had even gone to Mr Halliwell's home in Leicestershire early in his post, when Mr Halliwell needed some papers fetching urgently.

Mohal took bags or papers to the MP's car, or a meeting, or a committee room. Apart from the office, he rarely got through the door to join the gathering, unless he chose to watch as an observer to proceedings or debates, sitting with other members of the public. More usually, while Mr Halliwell conducted Parliamentary business Mohal sat outside in the corridor, like a faithful hound, and used the time to chat to Departmental officials and political advisers. These included Sebastian, Mervyn Halliwell's Special Political Advisor (or 'SPAD' as Mohal tells Rita they are known). Sebastian always carries a smartphone and holds his iPad on his arm as if it were a file that he may need to refer to at any moment. While talking to Mohal about his career to date, Sebastian, only three or four years older than the student, was constantly checking Twitter and various political blogs as well as updating Facebook and tweeting on Mervyn Halliwell's behalf. Mohal was envious and had aspirations to be a Sebastian one day, but he knew how hard it would be without connections and an independent education; he went to a state school and his parents make their living in dentistry, not in politics.

Mohal saw other figures hovering around his boss. As well as his own team, Mervyn Halliwell, as a Minister in the coalition, had Departmental officials who accompany him to Parliamentary and Committee debates and had briefing meetings with him, either at the House of Commons or in the Department. The Department is forbidden territory to Mohal, his pass will not take him there, but he has talked to a fast track HEO ('Higher Executive Officer' he explained when Rita asked) from the Department whom he found himself sitting next to one long Thursday afternoon. The

Committee proceedings of a Bill which Mr Halliwell was helping to promote had been interrupted on several occasions by whipped votes in the Commons ('That's when their parties say they have to vote a particular way' Mohal told his sister, pleased to be able to pass on this newly acquired information). Mohal, who had been sitting outside the committee room in the corridor, surrounded by extra briefing material in lever arch files should Mr Halliwell need it, had been entertained to hear the Division bell ringing repeatedly and to see MPs on the Committee, including his own boss, scurrying down the corridor, pulling on jackets, checking their phones, tidying their hair and, for the women, their handbags, as they rushed along to the voting lobbies with all the intensity of health professionals in search of a crash trolley. The heart of democracy had required constant attention that day to keep it beating.

Nigel, a Communications Officer in the Communities Department, had told Mohal, on another occasion when he was waiting in the corridor, how he got his job. He said that he had not sought such a post originally but drifted into the Civil Service having failed to get into the City – for which he blamed the recession - "Bad timing" he had said "They were laying off investment bankers when I was looking, not taking them on." He had described the laborious recruitment process – he had taken various tests, filled in forms, attended a day of interviews and role plays and then waited about six weeks before being advised of his appointment. "The pay's rubbish, I couldn't afford to do the job if my parents didn't live within commuting distance. My parents live in Twickenham so I travel from there. You have to be central." he had added "There can be long hours especially when there are problems with a debate or a Bill." Nigel could not be stopped once he had embarked on the relative merits of his job. "The Ministers don't treat you well, or not very often; they can be very off-hand, so it's a pretty thankless task – literally!"

Nigel had told Mohal he had hoped to be fast-tracked for promotion but "Things aren't what they were. Opportunities are few and far between. All the Departments are going through restructuring exercises and HR expect managers to find that 10% of the workforce are 'unsatisfactory' each year." Nigel had said he thought he'd stick it out for a couple of years and then try the City again. "The Civil Service is not a long term career any more." he had said. This had spurred on Mohal to consider taking the political adviser route. Who knew, maybe one day he would stand for Parliament himself, he fantasised.

"So what are you doing with the holiday?" Mohal had asked Rita.

"I have some driving lessons but I literally don't know when." she said, "I've not checked my online diary yet. My head was so full with getting rid of the parents and Nayan… Oh yeah," she said, looking at her iPad notes. "4pm tomorrow driving lesson with Mr Patel."

"No relation." the siblings said in unison.

"Goodoh. Maybe he'll let me go on the dual carriageway soon." Rita had been eager to do more than check her mirrors and practise with the gears.

"Don't be in too much of a hurry," her brother advised, "You have to learn bit by bit." he added his voice of experience. "And the weather forecast isn't great. Storms are on their way. Don't get wrapped round a tree, there have been several accidents in the news."

"Yeah, but I do want to get on with it, and he's so cautious… 'check this', 'check that'." she mimicked.

"Well, there's a reason." said Mohal, sounding like his father, then "Booked your theory test yet?" he asked.

"Nah. Thought I'd do it over the next holiday." Rita replied.

"Get it booked soon. Make sure you get a good slot. Don't want to have to get up too early for it." Mohal added with feeling. All the family have been amazed that Mohal can get up in time for his job with Mr Halliwell; he is not a morning person.

"Enjoy the peace and quiet." Mohal had signed off, "And don't do anything I wouldn't do!"

"As if!" Rita had rejoined.

* * *

Now Rita, sitting behind the steering wheel, tunes in again to the soothing tones of her driving instructor, Mr Patel.

"And neutral and handbrake." he adds patiently. Rita obeys, sees the police car poised behind them in her rear view mirror, and presses the switch to open the window on the driver's side so she can speak to an officer.

"No, no." Mr Patel admonishes her, "We are not in America, Miss Patel," he says.

"You need to get out of the car and speak to the policeman. Find out what he wants. Remember," he adds reassuringly, "You have done nothing wrong. No traffic violation at all."

Rita scrambles out of the vehicle, the car keys in her hand, flustered. She is confronted by a tall, red-haired figure in large sunglasses (which seem a little unnecessary in the damp autumn air), a green t-shirt, washed denim jeans and trainers. This is Inspector Jamie Bridge from the Leicester police. Rita knows him. She had been interviewed by him in connection with an unexplained death in the summer.

"Rita Patel," he greets her as they meet by the learner vehicle. "Priya said you'd be here." he adds, removing the sunglasses from his face.

Rita looks taken aback. Why is the Inspector here? And why has he been speaking to her best friend? Jamie Bridge tries to explain, "You're not answering your phone…There's some bad news I'm afraid."

"What?" says Rita, suddenly afraid for her parents and her younger brother, has something happened in India, she thinks?

"Your brother Mohal has been trying to get hold of you." the Inspector tells her.

"Why?" Rita cannot trust her voice to say more.

Inspector Bridge says slowly "I'm afraid he's been arrested. By the Metropolitan Police… in London… for murder."

Chapter

2

"No man is regular in his attendance at the House of Commons until he is married."

Benjamin Disraeli.

Tuesday, 22nd October 2013 4.30pm

Mr Patel is emerging from the driving school Corsa on the passenger side as Inspector Bridge delivers his news. Startled, Mr Patel drops the papers he is cradling in his arms as he climbs out. The white sheets flutter underneath the car like a flock of doves. The police driver, who conveyed Inspector Bridge along Aylestone Road in pursuit of Rita, steps out of their car on the driver's side, and strolls over to help Mr Patel retrieve his papers.

"I don't understand." Rita manages three words to Inspector Bridge, standing facing him on the driver's side of the car as her instructor and the other police officer scrabble for Mr Patel's papers under the wheels of the Corsa on the kerb side.

Jamie Bridge tries again. "I'm afraid Mohal's been arrested by the Metropolitan Police." he tells Rita, then "I gather your parents are abroad? If you come with us I'll tell you about it on the way to the police station. Then you can decide what you want to do… If that's alright with you, sir?" he adds, addressing Mr Patel, who stands up, clutching his papers to his chest to prevent them escaping again.

"Oh yes, officer." he says, "See you tomorrow for your lesson Rita." he adds, thinking to himself, as he does so, that this may be doubtful in the circumstances. Rita nods and hands him the keys, then retrieves her Cath Kidston bag from the back seat of the Corsa.

Rita has never been in a police car before. She sits in the back ('It looks like I've been arrested' she thinks) and Inspector Bridge turns round in his seat at the front to talk to her; he has put his sunglasses back on, despite the spots of rain hitting the windscreen, so his expression is hard to gauge. As he talks, Rita checks her phone (6 missed calls! 3 unknown number, 3 from Priya. What can have happened?). Rita thinks back over the last two days to see if there is a clue but nothing occurs to her.

"It's Mohal." Inspector Bridge explains as his colleague takes the opportunity of the next traffic lights to do a U-turn, sounding the siren for a few seconds.

"What's gone on?" Rita finds she is trembling now. "Did you say murder? What's he supposed to have done?" she adds, defending her brother automatically.

"The Met called us. I thought his name rang a bell from when you and I met in the summer. When they said Mohal couldn't contact his family I said I'd try to track you down. I had your number and Priya's from our previous meeting."

"Okay." says Rita as the police car is directed towards Leicester police station. "Our parents are away in India" she explains "…so what are the Met accusing my brother of?" she asks Jamie Bridge pointedly. ('Has Mohal run someone over perhaps, or is it a case of mistaken identity?' she thinks.)

"I'm afraid it's not looking good." Inspector Bridge says, shaking his head. "He's been arrested for the murder of his boss, the MP, Mervyn Halliwell. News of his death has been embargoed for security reasons, but there are rumours on the internet and Twitter already. The news will be released in about an hour," he says, looking at his watch. "It's standard procedure to hold off for a while when national security might be affected."

"National security? What are you talking about? I don't understand." Rita finds the trembling she was feeling has stopped and now she seems numb and as if there is a distance between her and the rest of the world, as if everything Jamie Bridge is saying is coming from a long way away.

"Look Rita," Inspector Bridge takes off the glasses again and turns a bit more to look Rita full in the face, "It's my job to investigate the bad guys. Not that I think Mohal is one you understand. I keep an open mind. But obviously what I tell you now I tell you because it's what you need to know, not because I believe it necessarily, you understand?"

"Yeah" Rita says quietly, her throat constricting.

"Okay. So don't shoot the messenger?" he adds.

"I won't." says Rita.

"We had a call from Scotland Yard. They say Mohal was at Mr Halliwell's office and that the MP has been stabbed to death. There's no sign of the weapon. They are questioning your brother now. That's about all I know."

Rita lies back against the car seat and breathes in and out slowly. ('How can the world out there, outside the car, be carrying on the same when this terrible thing has happened?' she thinks.)

The car is reaching its destination. They go down a slope to an underground car park. Rita realises Jamie Bridge is speaking again, "I shouldn't say, but I suggest Mohal needs a lawyer, and I think the Met would prefer that too. They need everything done by the book. I can put you in touch with your brother when we get inside and you can get the ball rolling."

"Thanks." Rita says, her head starting to teem with thoughts as the paralysis of the last few minutes wears off. (Who should she call? What should she say?)

"Of course I hope for your sake he hasn't done it." Jamie Bridge puts in. "I take it this comes as a total surprise to you?" he adds looking fixedly at Rita.

"Oh yes." says Rita not noticing his gaze as the driver proffers some ID to the security guard and steers into the parking area.

"The last thing I expected when I woke up today. Mohal was enjoying his internship with Mr Halliwell. He was finding the political stuff interesting, and he enjoyed the MP's surgeries." she tells the Inspector.

As the car is manoeuvered into a space and the three occupants walk to the lift and into the police station, Rita resolves to speak to her friend Priya as soon as possible, to get reassurance she is not going mad, then she will need to talk to Mohal to check he's alright and to say help is coming. Thirdly she decides to call Edward Maitland. Rita got to know him in the summer. He is a solicitor and, although he does not have a criminal practice, he will know someone who can help, Rita thinks. Then she will need to speak to her parents and, after that, her aunt Jaina; once she has made her call to her parents in India, Rita knows her mother will be on the phone to her sister.

Rita had assured her Aunt Jaina on the telephone only yesterday that 'she was perfectly fine thank you and enjoying the peace and quiet'. Now she cannot believe she will have to explain how much trouble Mohal is in. Yesterday she had been restless in the house in Elm Drive and had found herself moving from room to room in the solitude as if by doing so she could make it feel as though there were other people in the house. Now she has more to do than she can imagine and so many people to contact.

As soon as she can when she gets inside the station, and while Jamie Bridge is setting up the call with her brother, Rita finds a spot to sit by a window and as the rain starts to hurl itself at the glass,she scrolls through her phone to find Priya's number.

"Hi, what's up?" Priya responds, "I'm just helping Mum with some orders."(Priya's mother runs an internet clothing business from home).

"Oh" Rita is disappointed that her friend sounds too

busy to hear her news but she need not have worried. "Did Inspector Bridge get hold of you?" is Priya's next comment, "He sounded like it was pretty urgent!"

Rita explains that she is at the police station and that Mohal is in trouble. She is waiting to talk to him on the telephone.

"What kind of trouble? What do you mean?" Priya asks.

"I don't know how to tell you," says Rita, "They think he killed him, killed Mr Halliwell the MP!"

"What are you talking about?" Priya sounds alarmed. 'Has Mohal managed to poison someone with his cooking perhaps?' is all she can think. As she talks to Rita she is walking into her parent's room, where her mother is crouched over a laptop on the desk which doubles as a dressing table; Priya waves at her urgently, signalling that something is wrong.

"Oh dear!" Rita finds her voice wavering as her friend's concern communicates itself to her. "Inspector Bridge told me in the police car. He's being held at Scotland Yard. The facts are that Mohal says he found Mr Halliwell earlier this afternoon, in a locked room at Portcullis House in London, the place near Westminster where MPs have offices. Mohal says he was dead when he found him." she pauses "But the police say they only have Mohal's word for that." she goes on falteringly.

"Dead how?" Priya asks, shocked.

"Stabbed." Rita replies.

"With?" Priya queries monosyllabically.

"They are waiting for the post-mortem." Rita answers. She is finding it easier to speak while her friend asks factual questions. "There was no weapon at the scene…That's about all I can tell you."

"And you're at the police station now?" Priya checks, "In Leicester?"

"Yeah." Rita says hoarsely.

"Don't worry Rita." says her friend, "I'm sure it will be

okay, but Mum and I will come now. We'll come to help you!"

* * *

Half an hour later, Rita is with a female police officer and otherwise alone in a room which is empty except for a table, two chairs and a telephone. The police say Rita needs someone with her for Mohal's call as she is under 18. Rita thinks they may have another motive; she imagines that whatever she and Mohal say will be noted. As she imagines this, she recalls with horror the discussion she and her elder brother had on Sunday, when they were talking about Nayan and whether he had managed not to say 'bomb' on the plane. ('The police would not have listened to that would they? You hear all sorts of stories about calls being monitored.' Rita thinks, then decides to put the idea out of her mind.)

"Oh Rita!" Mohal on the police telephone sounds distressed and not like himself at all, his voice is weak and his tone pleading. "You've got to help me. None of it makes sense. There was blood, on my hands, I didn't know what to do!"

"Slow down Mohal!" Rita tries to calm her brother, "You don't have to tell me anything and you don't have to talk to the police until you get a solicitor." she tells him. "You've had a shock. You need to calm down."

"I know, I know!" he wails, "But you can't imagine what it's like, they've taken my clothes and my fingerprints and a DNA sample. They think I did it Rita!" Mohal says in desperate tones.

"Now listen," Rita tries again, "Don't worry. I'll get a lawyer on the case and all this can be cleared up. It must just be a horrible mistake."

"Okay, and the parents?" Mohal asks.

"I'll make sure they know. Don't worry. If you need anything get them to let you call me. And by the way,

24

Inspector Bridge from the Leicester Police is involved too – you remember I met him in the summer – so you can get a message to me through him."

"I have to go now." Mohal is breathing more easily than when their conversation began Rita is pleased to note.

"Okay, well take it easy and don't worry. We'll soon sort this mess out." Rita reassures him.

"Thanks Rita." Mohal gulps a little as if there is a lump in his throat.

Chapter

3

"I see all the birds are flown."

King Charles 1st (4 January 1642
when he marched into the
House of Commons to arrest 5 members
and found they had escaped)

Tuesday, 22nd October 2013 5.30pm

I witnessed your misguided kissing in the Strangers Bar in the Commons, and was subjected to your drunken fumblings in Soho bars; I watched you go too far at alcohol fuelled parties at political conferences, yet you hid your predatory nature well, everyone thinks of you as a 'good egg' don't they? But I never thought....

Do you know what you did to me at your constituency home? How powerless I felt? Like Houdini without a padlock key. No means of escape. You had taken away my power, my ability to control what was happening to me. Maybe I will grow a beard. Or I might get a tattoo. I will try anything to make me look and feel different, because, thanks to you, I no longer want to look and feel like me.

So today was the day for my revenge and you didn't even know it! I wonder how long before it gets on the internet and the television. I expect they will eulogise you at first, when the news comes out; I wonder why it is taking so long, by the way. But eventually the truth about you will come out!

* * *

"You were telling me yesterday about Simon de Montfort and Parliament." Priya says when they are finally in Mrs Shah's car, being propelled to Elm Drive from the police station. The windscreen wipers are swishing across and back with mesmeric rhythm, scarcely clearing the rain which is falling fast from a dark sky. Priya thinks it will do Rita good to think about something else for a change and that her friend won't want to discuss Mohal in the hearing of Priya's mother.

"Oh yeah," Rita switches her brain from worry about her brother and what her parents will say, "de Montfort was a strong character, charismatic but dictatorial, probably a bit of a bully, certainly forthright and not tolerant of fools."

"A bit like a modern politican then!" Priya says.

"In some ways, yes. He is sometimes called the Father of the House of Commons, and he was interested in diluting the King's power, but you couldn't say he stood up for the Commons as we know it today. He was friends with the King, Henry III, for part of his reign and fought for him. But Henry was thought of as weak, and he was scared of de Montfort," Rita goes on, "The King said, when they met in a thunderstorm - the weather a bit like today's I guess - let me see," Rita consults her iPad notes and puts on a low growling voice "'By God's head, I fear you more than all the thunder and lightning in the world!'"

Priya laughs. "Wow! Must have been a difficult man!" she puts in.

"I think he probably was. You wouldn't want to argue with him. But we haven't got to him yet." Rita puts her friend straight. "Well Magna Carta, which was sealed in 1215, came about because the barons took on King John. One of the things it did was make the King subject to the law, something they did not have elsewhere in Europe, and Magna Carta said that the King couldn't raise taxes without agreement. So

Parliament had to meet for the King to get agreement for taxation, and Parliament also started to make law in the form of statutes. But all that took time."

"So Simon de Montfort came later?" Priya interjects.

Rita pauses to check the notes she made on the subject. "Yeah. Henry III, King John's son, was nine when he became King and he assumed power from his regent in 1227 - that's 12 years after Magna Carta was sealed- when he was only 19 years old."

"Wow!" Priya is in awe of such self assurance.

"Exactly!" Rita replies, (19 is roughly the same age as Mohal and she cannot imagine her brother in charge of the country).

"As well as being young he was more of a pious man than a soldier. He wanted to follow the example of Edward the Confessor. That explains why he was considered weak." Rita adds, looking at her notes again.

"Henry struggled with the barons – a sort of continuation of the arguments his father had that led to Magna Carta - and eventually Simon de Montfort took over power."

"Yeah, how did that happen?" Priya is amazed.

Rita warms to her theme. "Well, not only was Henry III a laid-back King, the English barons decided they didn't like him because he was French, and he had French courtiers and advisers, who he paid. The influence of the French advisers and their demands for more money were resented by all the people. Matthew Paris, the monk at St Albans, wrote in the sixth year of Henry's reign that people who did not speak English were held in contempt by everyone." Rita goes on, staring out of the car windows but not seeing the storm or the vehicles battling in it, she is lost in her historical imaginings.

"Henry tried to get the barons to meet him in Oxford but they refused because the 'aliens' - the French courtiers – would be there. They threatened to replace Henry – which Henry thought was offensive, he believed he was divinely appointed - and he had to stand by as they confiscated land from the French advisers. But worse followed. In 1258 the King needed money because he had paid a large sum to the Pope so that his son, Edmund, could be King of Sicily. His timing was bad as the harvest of 1257 had failed and the country was suffering a famine." Rita pauses at last.

"So basically Henry just didn't get it? How his people were suffering and couldn't afford him to be paying money to the Pope? But when is Simon going to turn up?" Priya manages a few words as she takes her comb from her bag to put through her hair.

"Patience," says Rita, "The barons bargained with the King and chipped away at his power. They said the French courtiers should leave and then they arranged a committee which proposed the king be directed by a council nominated by the barons; this was known as the Provisions of Oxford. The council took over conduct of the state and the Great Seal."

"Wow!" says Priya, "Henry really messed up!"

"Mmmn." replies Rita, "But it didn't work for long. The council members couldn't agree among themselves, and the idea was flawed because foreign policy at that time relied on the relationship between kings. So Henry was back in charge after two years, the Pope let him off the debt and he moved into the Tower of London to show his power, and also for protection."

"And Simon de Montfort?" Priya sighs to remind her friend.

"Yes, this is where he comes in. Worrying about the French advisers and fearing a foreign army, the barons asked Simon de Montfort to lead them in their fight to have an English monarch who was native-born. Of course the irony was that, although he was Earl of Leicester, de Montfort was French born and of a French family. His claim to the title had been recognised by Henry when they were friends, Simon fought for Henry in Normandy and that was his reward. He even married Eleanor, the King's sister, although the other barons weren't happy about that. For a while they had got on Okay, Henry needed Simon's fighting abilities and Simon needed Henry's influence. But Simon wanted Henry to have less power, so they ended up on opposite sides."

"Crazy times!" Priya interjects.

"So Simon took up the cause of the Provisions of Oxford on behalf of the barons. He sailed across from France." Rita goes on.

"He wasn't even here?" Priya is incredulous.

"He went back and forth I think. It was common to have lands in France and England in those days."

"Did he and the King end up fighting?" Priya asks.

"You bet," Rita confirms, "De Montfort was strong in London but Henry's son, Edward, who was more of a fighter than his father, had some successes against the rebels in a few places. Then there was a battle between de Montfort and Edward at Lewes in Sussex and de Montfort won. He shut Edward up in the local priory. The people seemed to side with the barons, there was a song of Lewes which went 'Common it is said, as the king wishes, so goes the law; the truth is quite otherwise, for the law stands, though the king falls.'"

"They were getting used to the idea that they didn't need a King?" Priya asks.

"Mmmn. They brought Henry to London and put him in St Paul's Cathedral. Nine barons under de Montfort took over power. So he was the first person in English history to seize power from the king and rule in his place. He called knights and burgesses – basically freemen - to join the advisory council, so he started the idea of having aristocracy and commoners on the council. But although there was a council, like I said, de Montfort was a tyrant and took all the power to himself, which is why you can't really say this was

Parliament taking power from the King, but it was a start." Rita goes on.

"What happened in the end?" Priya wants to know, but her mother has turned into Elm Drive and Rita puts down her iPad to search for her house keys.

"De Montfort died in a battle at Evesham and Henry got his power back. But he didn't undo the changes which started with the Provisions of Oxford, so from then on there was a Parliament with representatives of the aristocracy and what you could call common people. The basis for our House of Lords and House of Commons." she hurriedly tells her friend as they climb out of the car and go into her home.

* * *

"Poor Mohal." is the first thing Priya says when the girls are installed on the pink duvet cover in Rita's bedroom where she has retreated for safety and comfort. "How is he bearing up?" While Priya continues to comb through her long brown black hair, Rita is wondering if she has done all she can to help Mohal at the moment. Mrs Shah had sat in on the few questions which Inspector Bridge had put to Rita at the police station after her conversation with Mohal and Rita recalls those questions now, questions to which the answer was a careful 'no'. (Did Mohal have any strong religious or political beliefs? Did he have any friends or associates that Rita thought worthy of police attention? Did he own a knife? Had he visited a mosque? What kind of question was that?! Surely they knew the family were Hindu?). Mrs Shah has now gone to buy some provisions so she can cook a meal ("If you feel like eating?") before she takes Rita back to her house ("I don't think you should be on your own.")

"Hard to tell how he is," Rita tells Priya, "he sounded a bit in shock."

"Well not surprising! Duh! OMG he finds his boss dead,

31

and then he's accused of it? In public? What about his arrest?!" Priya is waving her arms around now in agitation.

They had put the television on when they arrived at the house, only to witness pictures of Rita's brother being pinned to the ground in the middle of Victoria Embankment in London. They found this quite disturbing; across the internet and on news channels there were films, taken on mobile phones by people going past the scene. Mohal was splayed on the ground, his face pressed into the concrete, his hands behind his back, at a pedestrian crossing where the traffic lights kept changing but no cars were moving, all traffic having been stopped by the police, security guards and police surrounding Rita's brother. He seemed to be lying at the foot of Big Ben, the camera angle foreshortened the distance from the other side of the road, and when the cameras panned round in the other direction there was an incongruous view, in the middle distance, of the giant white wheel which was the London Eye.

"Yes, Priya." Rita says, thinking to herself 'What can I do about it?'

"What happens next? They look for evidence? Then they release him?" Priya asks.

"Well that would be good." says Rita, "But the lawyer-"

"Who did you speak to?" Priya wants to know.

"You remember Edward, Athena's husband, from the Sundial bed and breakfast, where we worked in the summer? He's a lawyer so I spoke to him and he put me on to Tim Beresford in their practice, who does criminal work. Mr Beresford is in touch with a London agent who's been with Mohal for his questioning. Mr Beresford will go to London tomorrow." Rita explains.

"Tomorrow? He won't be released today?" Priya's voice rises as she speaks, her distress evident.

"Oh no, Mr Beresford didn't think so. The police have said they want to hold him overnight at least." Rita tells her friend absentmindedly as she mentally ticks off her 'to do' list.

"At least?!" Priya is outraged. "How long can they keep him like that?"

"It kind of depends." Rita tells her friend. "According to Mr Beresford it's 24 hours for a normal case, and that can be extended to 36 hours if a Superintendent decides it's necessary and 96 hours if they go to court for an extension."

"96 hours!" Priya is aghast, "But that's…that's…four days!"

"Yeah…but there's more. If they think it comes under the terrorism powers…"

"What?! What do you mean?" Priya cannot believe what she is hearing.

"If they can say it's terrorism related – well obviously Mohal isn't involved in anything like that, but you can see it from their point of view… a dead MP… Well, anyway, if they can argue that the terrorism laws apply, then the period is up to 14 days before they have to release or charge him."

"OMG!" Priya is horrified, "Can they keep him for two weeks? What counts as terrorism then?"

"As far as I can remember, from what the Inspector told me, it's an action or threat – in this case serious violence - designed to influence the government or an international government organisation or to intimidate the public, and done to advance a political, religious or ideological cause." Rita takes a deep breath as she finishes reciting this from memory.

"Mohal doesn't have a cause!" Priya is indignant. Then she has another thought "Where will they keep him?" she fears for Mohal now, will he be safe?

"He's in police cells at the moment, when he's not being questioned, they may move him to a more secure place, at Belmarsh Prison I think Mr Beresford said."

Priya exhales slowly, it is worse than she thought and her hopes for Mohal's early release are escaping like the breath from her body. Rita rattles on, unable to stop now she has started, just saying the words helps to start to make some sense of what is going on and what she has heard in the last few hours.

"The agent says they are going over everything – Mohal's phone, his contacts, his friends, the sort of questions Inspector Bridge asked me. They seem to think he's part of some extremist network. They are looking for the political, religious or ideological cause I guess." Rita tries to explain the way the police are thinking.

"That's crazy." Priya states her view.

"I know. Anyway, 'no freeman shall be taken or imprisoned … except by the lawful judgment of his peers.'" Rita recites.

"Where's that from?" Priya asks.

"Magna Carta."

"Oh yeh" says Priya, "You've seen that haven't you?"

"Yep. The first copy I saw was when I went to St Albans Abbey in the summer. Remember when my family went to visit Mohal at his student house in Hertfordshire? It was on loan to them from Lincoln Cathedral. Magna Carta (it means Great Charter you know) was sealed in 1215, when King John was around, so before Simon de Montfort came along, but it was the first time the barons got the better of the King. There was a preliminary meeting to discuss the idea of it at St Albans Abbey in 1213. So they were observing the 800 year anniversary of that meeting. There are four copies of Magna Carta left altogether – it's quite small really considering how significant it is, just one sheet with lots of Latin in tiny writing, and some of the Latin is in abbreviations. I've seen the one in Salisbury Cathedral too; the other two copies are in the British Library. I want to see them all!" she brightens when she tells her friend this. (On her favourite subject of history again Priya notes, trust Rita to find some old document to quote.)

"I expect the law's a bit more up to date than that." Priya ventures.

"Well, yes, but it's great to think it started so long ago isn't it?" Rita is still pleased to have found this historical reference. It makes her feel that Mohal will be safe; however long the police want to keep him, there will have to be a judicial process to decide if he can stay in custody or be released she feels sure.

"Oh, hang on, that's not your mum back already is it?" Rita has heard the doorbell. She leaves the bedroom to descend the spiral staircase which her mother Padma had put into the house ("To free up space!" she says; her husband, Jahi, thinks, yes but how difficult it is now if they want to take furniture upstairs!) Priya keeps Rita's bedroom door open so she can hear who it is at the front door. "Let me know if I can help!" she calls down to her friend.

Rita opens the door to find Inspector Bridge, minus his sunglasses and now in a light jacket, dampening in the rain, on the doorstep, together with two uniformed police officers, a white man and a black woman, both rather overweight she notes.

"Hello again, Rita, sorry about this." Jamie Bridge says. "I'm afraid we have a warrant to search this house." He produces a piece of paper. Rita doesn't really understand what it says and can't recall if Magna Carta has anything to say on the subject but she trusts Inspector Bridge ('That's probably why they sent him,' she thinks.) so she lets them in.

"We'll try not to make a mess." Jamie Bridge reassures her as the three enter the house. Rita looks down at their shoes, thinking how fastidious her mother, Padma, is about the carpets, and Jamie Bridge, noticing her glance, starts to take off his boots, indicating to the other officers to do the same. For a second the hall is filled with the comical sight of three police officers each balancing on one leg while they remove their shoes. It looks like a party game, or a Beryl Cook painting, as their large frames fill the hallway. But this is a serious business Rita reminds herself.

"If you show us Mohal's room and any computers in the house? That's really what we need to see. Unless we turn up anything suspicious."

'Suspicious? What could be suspicious in their house at Elm Drive?' Rita thinks. She also recalls, with relief, as she shows Jamie Bridge and the two officers up the staircase to the room at the front which is hers, that she left her Cath Kidston bag with her iPad in it on the back seat of Priya's mum's car, so they can't take that away! "Hello Miss Shah." Inspector Bridge greets Priya who is standing by the window in Rita's room, looking down on the street and the police car sitting under the light of the street lamp. ('The neighbours will have seen that,' Priya is thinking; 'they'll be wondering what's going on.')

"How are you?" Jamie Bridge asks. "You are looking a bit drier than when I saw you last!" he adds referring to an incident in the summer when he had been chasing a suspect and Rita and Priya had somehow ended up in a lake.

"I'm fine." Priya replies quietly, looking down at the carpet; she is not sure she wants to see the Inspector in Rita's house.

Rita continues the tour, showing the police officers her parents' room and Nayan's, then, across the landing, Mohal's ensuite bedroom.

"Okay." Jamie Bridge appraises this room quickly. "You two have a look in here." He says to his colleagues. "I'll see what's in the rest of the house." he adds. The two uniformed officers begin to look round Mohal's bedroom.

Rita steps away and down the staircase, Inspector Bridge following. She shows him the kitchen (he whistles in appreciation when he sees it. "Gosh, you could get my whole flat in here!" he says. He notes the Xbox and says they will have to take that along with all the games. Rita says she does not mind but thinks her brothers won't be pleased. (She briefly imagines officers at the police station gaming on the

Xbox when they should be catching criminals and dismisses
the image after a smile to herself.)

In Jahi's study, Inspector Bridge takes great interest in the
computer, even though Rita's father only uses it for boring
work stuff like the accounts for their dental practice, and he
says they will have to take that too. "It should only be for a
couple of days." he says.

After a while the two officers descend with a few papers
and letters belonging to Mohal which they have put in plastic
bags and briefly show Rita. Then the police officers go out
into the garden ('what could be of any use there?' Rita thinks,
watching as they use the key, which is kept in the lock, to
open Jahi's garden shed. ('Was Mr Halliwell killed with
garden shears?' Rita thinks and starts to giggle to herself
although nothing about the situation is really funny).

"Inspector" the woman officer calls and Jamie Bridge
goes to see what his officers have found, emerging with a can
of white paint. "We'll need to take this too." he says, holding
up the can to show Rita ('so the police want to do some DIY
as well'? she thinks).

Soon after that they are leaving, struggling back into
their shoes and taking their spoils to their car, looking like
shoppers in the January sales. Priya, who has watched the
police depart from Rita's bedroom window, comes down the
stairs to join her friend in the hall.

"They are taking this very seriously," she says quietly.

"I suppose they have to," says Rita, "But that does not
mean we have to like it. Oh Mohal! I wish you could come
home!" she wails.

* * *

Tuesday, 22nd October 2013 7pm

Mrs Shah is in the kitchen at Rita's house – she has always

wanted to try it out 'It's like being in John Lewis' she thinks. She had arrived back bearing ingredients for stuffed peppers and vegetable kebabs plus frozen yoghurt for desert. ('How much does she think we can eat?' thinks Rita.) Rita and Priya are sitting with elderflower cordials in the living room, idly flicking through the TV channels to find something to distract them but wanting to avoid any news coverage. They settle on re-runs of *Glee*, which they find on the catch-up channel, while they discuss the relative merits of *TOWIE* and *Made in Chelsea* and speculate about the *X Factor* audition rounds and who might make it through boot camp. They both hope Sam Bailey from Leicester will do well, not because they like her but because they think they should show local allegiance. They also discuss whether Daniel Radcliffe is 'fit' since he started taking parts in stage plays and films other than *Harry Potter* and whether Frances, from Market Harborough, could win the *Great British Bake Off*.

After a while they run out of distractions and Priya says, "So Mr Halliwell was found in Parliament?"

"Well, in his office, which is next to Parliament." Rita expounds, "Mohal found him, that's why he's a suspect, you can't blame them, I suppose. He said he had blood on his hands."

"Why was Mr Halliwell there? Why was Mohal there?" Priya asks, not unreasonably.

"I gather Mr Halliwell had a meeting with a constituent – what they call a surgery - but it's nothing to do with medicine. He must have arrived early because Mohal said he arrived in plenty of time for the meeting and Mr Halliwell was already there and already dead."

"Hmm." says Priya, "Funny thing, Parliament. I've never really understood what it was all about. Was that in Magna Carta too?"

"Well." says Rita, grateful to have some more history to think about instead of Mohal's plight. "Parliament comes from the French word for 'to speak'…"

"French again!" Priya exclaims. "That's what de Montfort was trying to stop!"

"Sort of, I guess," Rita agrees, "But after the Normans came, French was the language of the court for a long time so it's not surprising that words had their origins in French. The first use of the word was in 1236; 'parleys' were referred to in France in the 1230's as formal discussions between the King and his principal subjects."

"From Henry III things centred on Westminster Palace, which he loved, and developed. There are ceiling tiles from his time in the medieval section of the British Museum – they are beautiful! Henry built Westminster Abbey as we know it today, too. Parliamentary records started to be kept in the 16th century – Henry VIII's time, when the House of Commons took over St Stephen's chapel, which was deconsecrated; they have been meeting on the same site ever since. The fact there were Commons - not ordinary people then but Knights and Burgesses from each County - was a result of all the upset in Henry III's reign, remember, and Simon de Montfort. When Henry III got back into power he did not undo all the changes. So Parliament came to discuss the affairs of the King. Henry VIII decided not to live in Westminster, so the Lords took over the White Hall (Whitehall - get it?)" Rita glances at Priya, sprawled on the opposite side of the sofa.

Priya smiles at her friend. "But Parliament didn't stay there? It was burnt down by Guy Fawkes?" she asks.

"No, silly, the plot was foiled. Under Elizabeth I and James I, Parliament was called more and more because the monarch needed money. Catholics in England were disappointed when the English defeated the Spanish as they wanted to have a Catholic King instead of James; this led to the plot in 1605 to set the place alight, which did not succeed. Then James's son, Charles I, fell out badly with Parliament."

"That's an understatement!" Priya puts in, recalling this

bit of English history.

"Yeah, so that led to civil war- cavaliers and roundheads - there were various battles around Leicester."

"Really? I didn't know that." Priya is interested.

"Oh yeah. Anyway, the king was tried and executed and Oliver Cromwell ruled with Parliament for a few years but he was not much more successful than the King. Charles II was restored in 1662 and then there was another hiccup when his brother James, who was due to succeed to the throne, was a Catholic. Parliament asserted itself and invited William and Mary to take over. That's when we had another important document, the Bill of Rights in 1689, which sort of followed on from Magna Carta, and gave Parliament more of a role in governing.Political parties started then too, the Whigs and the Tories" Rita goes on with her explanation while Priya tunes in and out of the Glee episode on the tv with its songs and manufactured stage-related strife.

"Parliament was mentioned as part of the constitution in the Act of Union in 1707." Rita says.

"With Scotland?" Priya clarifies.

"Yeah, that's right. The period under Queen Anne and all the German King Georges was largely about developing the role of the Cabinet and Ministers, who were all in the Upper Chamber, the House of Lords, and we had the first chap to be called a Prime Minister." Rita tells her.

"So it hadn't burnt down then?" Priya asks, sure there was a fire. Rita gives her an admonitory look.

"The 19th century was about representation – gradually giving the vote more widely." she says, continuing with the constitutional history.

"But not to women?" Priya recalls.

"No, not until the 20th century." Rita confirms.

"Typical!" Priya is indignant.

"There's a great picture in the National Portrait Gallery of Parliament in 1833, after the Great Reform Act of 1832, and before it burnt down in 1834." Rita finally concedes there was a fire.

"How did it happen?" Priya wants to know.

"Some workmen decided to burn wood in stoves under the floor, and it sort of got out of hand." Rita explains.

"Unbelievable!" Priya is surprised.

"Yeah. Lord Melbourne said it was, 'One of the greatest instances of stupidity on record.' They decided to rebuild it in an old style so it looks like it's been there for longer, Gothic they call it."

"Who's a Goth?" asks Mrs Shah, mishearing as the girls walk into the kitchen to tackle the meal she has prepared.

Rita has barely sat down when the phone rings, and she apologises as she takes the call, anxious in case there is news from Mohal. But it is just her mother for an update, which she provides, playing down the visit of the police and assuring her that Mohal has a good lawyer who will do all he can. No sooner has Padma rung off than Jaina, Rita's aunt, calls. Rita brings her up to date too, knowing the two sisters will also shortly be in contact, the relatives in India having good call rates if they use the internet; it is possible they may Skype or use Facetime, if the relatives can get it working.

Padma and Jaina are relieved to hear that Mrs Shah is taking care of Rita. It was agreed that Rita should travel to London to see Mohal and his lawyer the next day, and that Bandhu, Jaina's husband, would join her as soon as he could get out of work commitments. Padma told her daughter they were trying to get on an earlier flight from India but it was a busy time and they were having difficulties.

"Don't worry." Rita had assured her mother "I'm sure it'll be over soon and he'll be home." she said with more conviction than she felt. As she gets into the car with Priya, when their meal is over and the kitchen tidied to Padma's standard, Rita thinks she would like to speak to Mohal again to wish him goodnight, but she knows that is impossible.

Instead, before she gets into the guest bed at Priya's house she prays an evening prayer.

"Oh Lord kindly forgive my wrong actions done knowingly or unknowingly, either through my organs of action (hand, feet, speech) or through my organs of perception (eyes, ears) or by my mind. Glory unto Thee O Lord, who is the ocean of kindness."

Chapter

4

"The dreadful truth is that when people come to see their MP they have run out of better ideas."

Boris Johnson, 2003

Wednesday, 23rd October 2013 9am

I wish I could have seen your face, but then it wouldn't have been such a surprise, would it? And it would have been harder to get away. I expected more blood if I'm honest, maybe your heart stops beating it round? Biology was never my subject.

I would like to have seen your face when you found the paint on your driveway, too. You managed to keep it quiet I noticed. Good media handling there. And the car – you can't have enjoyed getting that scratch sorted. I wonder what you told the garage?

But you didn't take me seriously did you? You never did. That's why you had to die!

* * *

Wednesday, 23rd October 2013 10am

Mr Patel (no relation) draws up outside Priya's house in Loughborough as agreed on the telephone. Rita stows an overnight bag on the back seat as she gets in the car and starts to check her seat and mirrors.

"Can you drop me at the railway station afterwards please?" she asks.

"What am I? A taxi service?" Mr Patel asks rhetorically, nodding agreement at the same time.

"Now let's get some driving done." he says. Rita turns the

key, puts the car into gear and checks her rear view mirror, releases the handbrake and they set off, juddering a bit at first and then going more smoothly as she finds the rhythm of the engine.

"I expect the excitement of yesterday will have put you off a bit." says Mr Patel as they cruise at 27 miles per hour. He knows the general story but is keen to glean any more information as the news items have been sparse owing to the 'reporting restrictions'. All the press can say is that a 20 year old man is 'helping the police with their inquiries'. Rita, who lay awake last night worrying that a member of the family, or a friend, might let slip that Mohal is involved, even inadvertently, silently adds Mr Patel to the list of people who could disclose Mohal's identity to the world if he wanted.

"I was surprised you wanted a lesson today actually," he probes, then "You're drifting into the middle," he adds and gently nudges the steering wheel over to the left.

"We won't attempt anything too difficult today" he says. "Practice roundabouts I think. We'll take the ring road. There are plenty of roundabouts and traffic lights there." Mr Patel gives Rita a few directions.

"It's about the MP, then? Mr Halliwell? The one that's been killed?" he ventures when he thinks it's safe to interrupt Rita's train of thought. "So where was Mohal when it happened?" he adds.

That, thinks Rita, concentrating on the road ahead and not answering, is a good question.

* * *

Wednesday 23rd October 2013 11am

"Can you tell us anything that may have happened recently to Mr Halliwell that may cast light on this event?"

Camilla Matthews, until yesterday Mervyn Halliwell's

diary secretary, is having trouble focussing on the questions of Detective Superintendent Sharp while his Detective Sergeant looks on anxiously and intently as if Camilla holds the key (figuratively speaking) to her boss's murder. The room they are in at New Scotland yard is a drab box-like office from the 1970s. It overlooks Victoria Street, but no one inside would know that because the view is obscured by the thick blast proof curtains at the window and the effective double glazing. In keeping with the latest practice, the interview is being held around a sofa. That is to say, Camilla's large frame is perched uncomfortably on the edge of one of the hard, grey, sofas, while her two interrogators sit uncomfortably close to each other on the opposite sofa. A coffee table lies low between them. A female Constable stands in the corner, by the unused desk.

"I…er…well, you must have a record… it must be logged on your system?" Camilla's well-manicured hand has pushed her reading glasses onto the top of her head and they sit perched on a nest of highlighted, blonde hair. Camilla is well-known in the nail parlours and hair salons of the Pimlico area of London, which is where she lives in a Housing Association flat she shares with her mother. The flat is convenient for work and she enjoys taking her mother out to tea, on special occasions, at the Reubens Hotel (they used to go to the Goring but she feels it's got above itself since it was taken over by the Middletons for the Royal wedding) and for Christmas lunch at the catering college near Vincent Square.

The Detective Superintendent and Sergeant exchange quizzical looks. 'What is the woman talking about?' they are both thinking.

"You know." she goes on, "The car, the paint." Camilla, who lay restlessly in her bed last night, not able to close her eyes let alone sleep, is agitated now.

The Sergeant gets up, and beckons the Constable. "Cup

of tea for Miss Matthews." he says. He sits down next to Camilla, glancing at his Chief Inspector, telegraphing that the woman needs a sympathetic approach. They both know that the Security Services are drawing a blank on any extremist motive, Islamic or otherwise, as are the Anti-Terrorism branch, so a personal angle seems the likeliest motive at present.

"Now, you've had a shock, we understand that. Take your time. There's a cup of tea coming. Tell us about these incidents and we can check on our computers."

"I don't know why you don't know about them!" Camilla is indignant. "We told the police, reported it at once. Of course, Mr Halliwell wanted it kept out of the papers, but even so…"

"Well, why don't you just tell us?" the Detective Superintendent uses mollifying tones while exasperatedly pushing his hands through his mop of thick grey hair, which makes it stick up alarmingly and destroys any reassurance Camilla might have derived from his approach. The Detective Superintendent has also slept little since the murder and his face is almost grey with fatigue. In fact, none of the people in that room are at their best except for the Constable, who only returned to duty after a holiday that morning, and she has gone to fetch the tea.

"Which was first, the car or the paint?" the Detective Superintendent adds. Sergeant Kahn gives his boss silent credit for paying attention and recalling Camilla's words.

"The car," she says, "It was parked outside Mr Halliwell's home – the one in Oakham, in Leicestershire - that's where he lives, lived." As Camilla starts to break down, the Sergeant pushes the box of tissues on the coffee table towards her, just as the tea arrives.

"Drink this, Miss Matthews. It will make you feel better." says the Sergeant who is of a wiry build and balding and whose appearance vaguely reminds Camilla of the Conservative

MP Sajiv Javid. She reluctantly takes a sip.

The Detective Superintendent, who has smoothed down his hair and patted it flat again, takes up the story.

"So the car was parked outside Mr Halliwell's home in Leicestershire, in Oakham. On the pavement or the drive?"

"Oh, I'm not sure, but on the drive I would think. The house is set back from the road." Camilla supplies between sips. The tea is rather hot but is reviving her.

"And what happened to it?" the senior officer continues gently.

"When Mr Halliwell came back from London, he found there were scratches down the side. Deep scratches. Someone had done it on purpose, it couldn't have been an accident."

"And how do you know that?" the Sergeant asks her.

"Because the scratches spelt a word, in large capital letters, on the driver's side. It said 'DIE'" Camilla explains.

"And when was this?" the Sergeant speaks again.

"The day after that debate. The one they were recalled for back in the summer. About Syria?" Camilla Matthews looks at the men to see if they understand.

The Sergeant has his mobile phone in his hand and scrolls through to find a number as he walks away from Camilla.

"Hello, Inspector Bridge?" she hears him say then, as he waits, he covers the phone to ask Camilla "When was that debate Miss Matthews?"

"The end of August." she tells him "In the summer recess. The Government were defeated." she adds unnecessarily.

The Sergeant nods as if this is significant and leaves the room to speak to Jamie Bridge. Detective Superintendent Sharp encourages Camilla to sip more tea. Then,

"And the paint?" he asks, keeping one eye on the secretary and the other on his Sergeant whom he can see through the glass in the door.

"That was in October, around the time of the party conference, a Tuesday I think. I could tell you the date if you let me have my lap top back." Camilla suddenly asserts herself; she had been indignant when the police had taken away her computer yesterday, the one on which she kept Mr Halliwell's diary. ('As if that would help them!' she had thought).

"Mrs Halliwell was with him at the conference so there was no one at the Oakham house. Mr Halliwell… oh dear…"

"Take your time." The Detective Superintendent manages to say while glancing to see what's happening outside the room; where is Sergeant Kahn and what has he found out? He is impatient to know.

"Where was the paint?" he prompts.

"It was on the path, outside his front door. Large letters. Mr Halliwell took a picture. That's how I know. He emailed it to the police."

"What did it say?" DS Sharp asks patiently, although his voice is starting to belie him. Time is ticking by. They need to find out if they are dealing with a maverick individual, or a group? Was it a person with a grudge or a more sinister motive? Did the crime involve a political or religious or ideological cause, was there a security issue? Was anyone else in danger or under threat? All the top brass in the force had been hovering round the case, including Deputy Commissioner Alison Tate who was in overall command of the incident, there had been more braid at the morning briefing than at a Girl Guide meeting his Sergeant had said. They wanted results. Something to tell the Home Secretary. And all they have is Mohal Patel in custody proclaiming his innocence, and this blubbing woman.

"The paint said – it was white paint and large letters – DIE MERVYN. Do you think it's the same person?" Camilla asks as if she has just thought of it.

"Well, we'll look into it. You drink your tea Miss Matthews. We'll need to ask you some more in a minute."

The Detective Superintendent leaves the room to speak to

his Sergeant about any information from the Leicester police on the paint and car incidents, leaving the two women alone. Camilla absorbs the steam still coming from her cup – all tea comes superheated these days she had noted before, it was a result of the coffee shop revolution in the high street.

Sergeant Kahn and Detective Superintendent Sharp return. The Constable in the corner, who was slumping against the wall recalling her holiday, straightens herself up at their approach.

"Now Miss Matthews." says the Superintendent in his friendliest tones. "Tell us about Mr Halliwell's movements yesterday."

Camilla explains that Mervyn Halliwell was in a Committee at the House of Commons until 11.30. He was then due to have a meeting with a constituent.

"And the meeting was when?" Sergeant Kahn asks inclining his head forward; the timing of the events has become an important line of the inquiry.

"That's the odd thing." says Camilla. "When I printed the calendar off – I do that every evening for Sebastian, Mr Halliwell's political adviser, and for the intern, I'm sure it said 2.15 but when I looked online after... after... what happened," she pauses to catch her breath, "It was scheduled for 12.15."

"And you didn't change it?" DS Sharp asks.

"Oh no." Camilla confirms.

"Could Mr Halliwell or anyone else have changed it?" the Sergeant probes.

"Only Mr Halliwell had access to make changes, as well as myself. But he rarely did." Camilla explains.

"And who is the constituent he was meeting?" the DS leans forward.

"I'm afraid I don't know," Camilla shrugs, "The name is Maria Faridi, but I don't know who that is. I am not familiar with all Mr Halliwell's constituency business."

"Would you know how the meeting was arranged?" Sergeant Kahn again.

"I think by email, although I can't be sure. You can check on my lap top." Camilla cannot help sounding petulant, the laptop is (or was) an essential part of her professional life.

The officers assure Camilla that is what they will do. Then they want to know what work Mr Halliwell was involved in, can she tell them any issues he was involved in which might be controversial?

Camilla pauses to think. "Well in a way everything an MP does is controversial to someone isn't it?" she says at last. "That's the nature of politics. Not everyone agrees."

"Tell us about the Syria business then. How was Mr Halliwell involved in that?" DS Sharp knows that SO15 (Counter-Terrorism Command) are interested in that aspect, looking for an extremist connection.

"Well, I was just his secretary, you understand, you'd need to ask his Parliamentary colleagues about the details. But as far as I understand it, Mr Halliwell reluctantly supported the Government in the vote on intervening, but he had also been on a Treasury Committee which criticised charities claiming to help Syrian civilians when they were really arming the rebels, or so he said. Mr Halliwell made a few speeches about the naivety of some in the anti-Assad faction and he worried that people going to Syria to fight would come back as terrorists. Could that have made him some enemies, do you thnk?" she asks as she finishes her tea.

* * *

Wednesday, 23rd October 2013 2pm

Rita is on the train to London, hoping the police will let her see her brother tomorrow but she is not optimistic. Thinking about the journey and the challenges ahead she recalls a mantra to Ganesh who is known as the god of wisdom and the destroyer of obstacles.

"Om Gum Ganapatayel Namah", meaning "I bow to the elephant-faced deity [Ganesh] who is capable of removing all obstacles. I pray for blessings and protection."

At least she will get to talk to the lawyer, Tim Beresford, who is now staying in London and has been with Mohal for most of his interviews that day. Aunty Gee is expecting her and is ordering a take away as a welcome – she does not cook any more as arthritis has deprived her of full use of her hands. Fortunately her son, who lives with her, is a chef in a hotel near St James Park so he sometimes provides meals. He is on a long shift today but should be able to take Rita into London on Thursday and point her in the direction of Scotland Yard, Aunty Gee told her when they spoke ("What a terrible business! I cannot believe it! Lovely Mohal!").

Rita tries to sketch a time line but finds she has little information. Apart from 'Tuesday 22 October, 2pm, Mohal finds Mr Halliwell' what else can she put? Where was Mr Halliwell before that? Where was Mohal? If Mohal is innocent (which he is, she is sure) why did he not see anyone around when he went into the room? How did the killer get into the room? What are the security arrangements? All these questions teem through her brain like the rain drops running down the train window.

Rita stares out of that window, recalling her converstation with Priya about Magna Carta and thinking about the day she saw another copy. Jahi had attended a dentists' conference in Salisbury in September and she had gone along. He had dropped her in the town centre and she had walked through the old streets, decked with shops, through the cobbled market square and down to the Cathedral.

Salisbury Cathedral was as proud of having Magna Carta as no doubt Leicester Cathedral would be at having the remains of Richard III, Rita had thought as she walked along. "If they succeed in getting them" Jahi had said when Rita had mentioned this in the car on the way. "There's no guarantee and they have spent a lot of money getting ready for it." They both knew the Plantagenet Alliance was to bring proceedings involving the Ministry of Justice and the Cathedral to challenge the licence under which it was agreed that, if found, Richard's remains would be reinterred in Leicester Cathedral. Opponents argued that as the last Plantagenet King, and the last to die in battle, he would have wanted to be buried in York. 'That's as may be' Rita thinks, 'But the point is that he lost the battle so in a way he lost the right to say where he should be buried. After all, he was originally interred at Greyfriars in Leicester so that was the intention at the time of his death.' As she understands it, the organisation representing descendants of the Platagenets is likely to argue that the Ministry of Justice should consult them (and the most prominent member of this group would be the Queen of course). So all the plans are on hold while the court sits to listen to barristers putting forward arguments over the burial of bones hundreds of years old. (Recalling this on the train, Rita contrasts the situation with that of her brother for whom Tim Beresford is, she knows, already struggling to find a barrister to take his case on Legal Aid rates.)

Salisbury Cathedral was like a large but delicate white wedding cake with its unfeasibly tall and thin tower (the tallest in the United Kingdom, she knew). Set aside from the town centre with a meadow to one side, Rita had felt she was stepping into the famous Constable painting of it which she had seen. Very little seemed to have changed since then. The building stood tall amid an array of delightful old houses, their windows reflecting the autumn light.

Going inside she was greeted by a friendly face who expressed a wish that she would enjoy her visit. Walking around the hallowed space, Rita heard running water and found to her delight a large bronze and stone font in the centre with water continuously flowing out of it and deep words from the Book of Isaiah, in the Old Testament, written around the edge -

"Do not fear for I have redeemed you. I have called you by name you are mine. When you pass through the waters I will be with you. And through the rivers, they shall not overwhelm you."

Rita knew the document she sought was in the cloisters – the guide had explained that, but as she had time she took care to examine some of the monuments in the main part of the cathedral and was thrilled to light upon an effigy of Lady Catherine Grey, sister to Lady Jane Grey, the 'nine day queen' in 1553, who Rita knows was born in Leicestershire, at Bradgate Park. The monument is to Edward Seymour, nephew of Jane Seymour, Henry VIII's third wife and Catherine Grey's husband. Catherine lies above Edward, one of the guides told Rita, because of her royal connections.

Moving on round the building Rita had arrived at the cloisters – a square of corridors with open sides and grass in the middle. A modest sign pointed her to the Chapter House where the best preserved copy of the Great Charter lay. Rita was thrilled to read that in July the Chapter House had been the location for the launch of art work for Jay Z's album *Magna Carta. Holy Grail.* History and present day coming together! Jay Z had actually been to see it before he went to the Wireless Festival to join Justin Timberlake! She must tell Priya! She marvelled (again) at the small size of the canvas on which the historic words were written. Such a powerful document so compressed. And she admired the spidery script, in neat lines but too tiny to read- how did the clerks manage to write so small and in conditions without electric light? she wondered.

On the train to London, Rita recalls some of the statements "To no man will we sell, or deny, or delay, right or justice."

"No man will be taken or imprisoned, except by the lawful judgment of his peers or by the law of the land."

These were clauses 39 and 40 on the due process of the law. Rita clings to these for hope. Surely the police cannot detain her brother much longer?

Chapter

5

"The argument of the broken pane of glass is the most voluble argument in modern politics."

Emmeline Pankhurst

Thursday, 24th October 2013 11am

Thursday is a slow day for Rita, like being caught in a traffic jam and not being able to see the cause. Aunty Gee, with her long grey hair, struggling to manage with her walking stick and wearing her old fashioned sari, fusses over her at breakfast. "Eat more Coco Pops, you must keep your strength up." and Rakesh, her son, guides Rita on the journey from Neasden to St James Park. From there she is on her own to wander and wait; she takes a teabreak interrupted by a call from Tim Beresford, when he can snatch a moment in between Mohal's interviews with the police, and Rita and the lawyer plan to meet in Starbucks opposite the tube station at 11am. While she waits, Rita looks around nervously at the people on the other little green tables. How many of them have business with Scotland Yard she wonders?

To pass the time Rita calls Priya. They chat about the beautiful three tiered cake which had helped Frances Quinn win the *Great British Bake Off* – how imaginative she is! And such lovely colours! - And how composed Prince George seemed in his christening pictures.

"It's as if he knows what his role is already!" Rita says.

"Yeah, he'll be King and head of the Church of England one day, won't he? If it stays as the established religion." Priya asks.

"Yes," Rita confirms. "Ever since Henry VIII that's been

the case." Then she spots Tim Beresford striding towards the coffee shop. "Got to go! Ciao!"

"Bye, let me know how it goes!" replies her friend.

Mr Beresford is tall – at 6 feet four he is a couple of inches taller than Mohal - and he holds himself straight, demonstrating the years he spent in the military before qualifying as a solicitor. Although suited today, he has a fondness for army style jumpers which he likes to wear around the office when not in court or seeing clients and Rita has noted from their phone conversations his tendency to use upbeat phrases as if he is encouraging troops.

"Hello Rita." he greets her, settling his briefcase on the table in front of her, "Mohal will be glad to know you're here."

"How is he?" Rita asks, looking up at the lawyer who is examining the change in his pocket.

"He's doing fine." he reassures her. "Tea?" and he makes a drinking gesture. Rita agrees to try to ingest yet another mug of tea which Tim Beresford conveys to the table and then he appears to fold himself in half as he sits opposite Rita, placing his briefcase on the floor.

"Will they let me see him?" Rita inquires, trying not to sound too desperate but realising her voice sounds strained.

Tim Beresford shakes his head as he sips from the mug. He has left the tea bag in for a long time so the drink is almost orange in colour. A decent cup of tea is a welcome change to the endless and tasteless machine coffee which is all that is available at Scotland Yard.

"I doubt it, but I'll keep trying. Keep your chin up." he encourages her, "The police have various officers who want to talk to your brother, but to be honest there's not much he can tell them. My main task is to make sure he gets proper breaks, and meals! An army marches on its stomach!"

He changes tone then "You should be prepared though. I think they are getting ready to charge him."

"Charge him?" Rita almost drops her cup in shock.

"With killing Mr Halliwell?" she checks to make sure she has understood.

"I'm afraid so." Tim Beresford sighs and passes his free hand across his forehead.

"Mohal was there. He admits that. The blood on his hands belonged to Mervyn Halliwell anyway so there'd be no point in denying it." the lawyer goes through the evidence.

"But just because he was there doesn't mean…" Rita protests, her voice disappearing in her throat as she pushes away her tea. Her stomach is churning and she cannot face another sip. She had been so hopeful that she would see her brother today, she had even hoped that the police would realise their mistake and let him go.

"I know." the lawyer sympathises. "Until all the forensics come through it's only circumstantial, but he's the only suspect they've got, he can't deny being there, and it looks suspicious that he ran from the building."

"But then he ran back!" Rita protests.

"Well." Mr Beresford sighs, looking into the bottom of his mug from which he has drained all the tea already. Sitting in on interviews is thirsty work! "Strictly speaking and from the police perspective, that's where he says he was going. The police look at this differently, and criminals do strange things, give themselves away in lots of ways. So I'm saying - shoulders back and be prepared.The police will have sent the evidence to the CPS - the Crown Prosecution Service - and they will evaluate whether charges should be brought. I think we'll know by this afternoon."

"Is there anything we can do to help him?" Rita begs. "Is there anything about his story that we can check out for him?" she asks, wanting to be helpful, hating this inaction, "Where does he say he was before, before the body was found?" she asks. Her only conversation with her brother has been the brief one on Tuesday and she has not heard the full story he is giving the police.

"He says he was at lunch on Victoria Street with no witnesses." Tim Beresford tells Rita.

"Won't there be CCTV evidence?" Rita asks, looking for hope.

"Well, people always think CCTV is the answer these days. Too much Crimewatch! The trouble is Mohal is vague about where and when he was exactly and the police won't trawl though hours of CCTV to look for him."

"What about appealing for witnesses?" Rita suggests, her voice lightening. 'Surely someone would remember her brother?' she thinks.

"Yes we could try." Tim Beresford puts down his mug and spreads out his hands as he explains to Rita, "But that would mean exposing Mohal. Putting his face on national TV. Do you want to do that? Do your parents? It's a tough situation."

"Hmmmn." Rita can see the point of what Mr Beresford is saying. Is there a way to clear Mohal which doesn't end up with his name and details across the internet and national media? she wonders.

"And anyway the police won't like it in all probability. They are playing the security card for all its worth." Mr Beresford adds.

"They can't think Mohal is a danger to security! That he did this – which he didn't - for some political or religious reason! He's not like that!" Rita is outraged on her brother's behalf. 'He may be lazy and cheeky but he is not a fanatic.' she thinks.

"You and I know that." Mr Beresford explains patiently, checking his phone for messages and emails. "Mohal has an hour's break until 12, then the lawyer must return for another team of police officers to question the young student.

"Well who else are they questioning? Do they tell you that?" Rita wants to know.

"Not directly, no, but I gather from questions they are putting to your brother that they've talked to the rest of Mr

Halliwell's staff. A Miss…" the solicitor consults his large blue note pad, "Matthews and a Sebastian… Stainer."

"What do they say?" Rita inquires, she recognises the names from conversations with her brother.

"Well, I am not privy to their statements but there seems to be an issue around a meeting, the time of a meeting, which Mr Halliwell was due to attend on the day he died."

Rita leans forward, this might be important! She is aware that the café is filling up and a few people are casting envious eyes at their table. Well, they will have to wait, she thinks. She has drunk enough tea to be entitled to stay for a bit longer!

"Tell me about it!" she demands.

"Mohal maintains he thought Mr Halliwell was meeting a constituent – I have her name somewhere but I don't think it's relevant. "Mohal thought…" the lawyer corrects himself, "Mohal tells the police he thought that the meeting was at 2.15. So he got to the office in plenty of time as far as he was concerned, arriving at the building around 1.45pm and going to the office at 2pm, as Mr Halliwell wanted him to attend."

"And?" Rita cannot see where the mystery is.

"Well, Mr Halliwell's secretary and Sebastian Stainer agree with Mohal, it was for 2.15, at least that was the case the prevous evening."

"There you are then!" Rita is indignant. Mohal is telling the truth. Why would he lie? she thinks.

Tim Beresford gives Rita a sharp look. It is understandable that she is taking the side of her brother. But part of his job is to look at the allegations from the point of view of the police and the CPS. How do the facts look to them? Once you assume everyone is lying, the kaleidoscope of events changes to form a new pattern. It was not that the lawyer is imagining conspiracy theories involving all of Mr Halliwell's staff, 'this is not Murder on the Orient Express' was one of his phrases, but one scenario is that they had agreed the time of the meeting together; they spent lots of time in each other's company after all. But why would they want to lie? Were they trying to implicate Mohal? Mr Beresford is puzzled.

"And?" Rita is still confused.

"Well, the police have the laptop of the secretary, Miss Matthews." Tim Beresford rustles through his note book again. Rita can see page after page of spidery notes illuminated every so often with his doodles of what look like spacemen in the margin, as if the interviews have been witnessed by creatures from another planet.

He continues, having found the reference, "The online calendar has the meeting down for 12.15 not 2.15. Your brother says he didn't have access to that, only a printed off copy which the secretary would give him the night before."

"So it got changed by a person online?" Rita is brightening. Now it looks like someone has deliberately set her brother up she thinks, following the same train of throught as Tim Beresford. Was it his secretary? Or Sebastian whatshisname?

"Maybe" Tim Beresford concedes, "That's a possibility. Or Mr Halliwell could have changed it himself." he points out.

"S'pose." says Rita deflated again. Then another idea occurs to her, "What if this constituent did it? They could have changed the time. Met the MP and stabbed him and left before Mohal arrived?" she puts forward.

"Yes, that's a good theory." the lawyer concedes, "Except that Mohal saw no one and nothing suspicious and the police cannot find the constituent, it's as if she doesn't exist." he goes on.

"It's a woman?" Rita clarifies.

"Oh yes." Tim Beresford confirms, rifling through his large blue notebook again, "Maria Faridi." he tells Rita.

"What did she want to talk about?" Rita wants to know next.

"Mohal had no clue. I gather a lot of people approach their MP on visa and asylum issues for example, so that's a possibility."

"And what if she was a fanatic? You remember that MP who was attacked with a sword?" Rita is agitated now, "A woman did that." she says emphatically as if this proves her theory.

"Well there's the small issue of the airline style security for visitors on their way into the building." the lawyer seems to pour cold water over her idea, "But it would help if the police could find the lady. Then we could learn more."

"Was she signed in? Did she arrive and leave before Mohal perhaps?" Rita asks.

"Apparently she's not in the visitors' register. Quite a few people visited that day but no one who sounds like her. The police are interviewing the security guards to see what they recall, and anyone they can identify who may have been in the building, but it's just routine really, I don't think they expect to find anything." he sighs, sorry to disappoint Mohal's sister.

"Can we investigate?" Rita is still keen, "Could we get a private investigator to look for her?"

"Well possibly we could," Mr Beresford sounds cautious. "But there are two problems with us taking action to investigate this case. One is the security aspect which we've mentioned, the police may prevent us revealing details of potential witnesses."

"Or suspects." Rita puts in.

"Or suspects." Tim Beresford concedes.

"The other issue is cost." he goes on, "It's all controlled by the Legal Services Commission, as Mohal gets Legal Aid, but it's a limited budget and they won't pay for fishing expeditions or wild goose chases." he says, mixing his metaphors.

"We can't do nothing!" Rita is exasperated and swirls her cold tea round, watching the dark brown stain spread around the white walls of the mug.

"What if the laptop was hacked into? By someone else altogether?" she suggests, the clouds in her mind clearing again.

"That's another theory." Mr Beresford sounds unenthusiastic. "The police have the laptop I gather." he adds, "I don't know what they can tell from that." he picks up his briefcase, placing his notebook in it. The lawyer stands up again, tall and straight, "I have to go now. Back on parade!"

"Give Mohal my love." Rita says, rising from her chair too. She needs some air, even if it is only the fume-filled atmosphere of a London street.

"I will." Mr Beresford promises, adding "And be prepared for a difficult day. I doubt they will let you see him and it's entirely possible that when I see you again this afternoon he will have been charged."

"I understand." says Rita and watches sadly as the lawyer exits the café to rejoin her brother in a faceless dreary interview room.

What can she do? Stepping out of the Starbucks and turning left towards St James' Park, Rita resolves to make a phone call. She is on a pedestrian crossing to the park when she gets through.

"Hello, Cynthia?" Rita says. "It's Rita Patel. I wonder if I could speak to Simon?"

As Cynthia fetches her son to the phone and Rita strolls along the paths that snake around the well-tended flower beds towards a blue bridge across the lake, Rita recalls the events of the summer which brought her into contact with the mother and son. While helping at a bed and breakfast establishment in Leicester, Rita had become involved in investigating the murder of a guest, an actor with a chequered love life. There had been uncomfortable scenes when his present and previous wives had come face to face at the B & B. Cynthia was the first wife and she and her husband had a son, Simon, who Rita also met at the bed and breakfast. The same age as Rita, 17, Simon has learning difficulties and is on the autistic spectrum. He had spent most of his time, even in company and at meals, playing computer games but Rita knows, from listening to Simon, and his mother's anxiety about it, that Simon also does some computer hacking. Who better to explain to her how it's done and what would be needed to hack into Mr Halliwell's diary and alter the meeting time?

Rita explains to Simon, when he takes the phone from Cynthia, that her brother is in trouble. He is being questioned by the police (she does not explain why) and a question has come up about computer hacking. Simon listens and asks technical questions as she describes Mohal's boss as having an online diary and queries how easy it would be for someone from outside to alter an entry?

Simon says there are many ways to get into a computer programme using hardware or software. He explains there are things called 'keyloggers' which record the activity of a computer user for example. The keylogger captures keyboard strokes so the user can gather information on logins and passwords for example. Once you had that information you could easily access a diary and change it, he tells Rita. "Similar devices are used legitimately by IT companies to remotely login to computers to fix problems." he adds.

"What does a keylogger look like?" Rita asks naively.

Simon chuckles. "It might be something you can see, like a USB device, but it's more likely to be a piece of software that the hacker introduces onto the computer. Keylogger software is freely available on the internet." he says to her surprise.

"Or a person might just write some code and introduce it into the computer, say via a computer game, what's called 'malware'" Simon goes on.

"And if it's malware can you find out who did it?" Rita asks next.

"That depends. The malware's source code may disclose enough information to identify where the person lives, for example. Some hackers want the person to send information to a specific email address, so they give themselves away."

Rita gets hopeful. "But better hackers would not make that mistake." Simon adds to deflate her. "The most you might be able to trace is the ISP."

"ISP?" Rita queries.

"Internet Service Provider. The provider may then disclose the hacker, if they can find out and it the police have the powers to ask. ISP's are very sensitive about confidentiality and government agencies intruding on their network, so they are not likely to be cooperative unless they have to be."

Rita sits on a bench in the park and listens as Simon seems happy to explain the background to her.

"Hacking isn't necessarily bad." Simon tells her, "Lots of people do it for good reasons. It was a term invented in the 1960s for people who wrote code. To that extent people like Steve Jobs were 'hackers'. Nowadays most people think only of the bad sort. But good hackers meet together and share information at conferences and online. That's how you can learn things." he goes on.

"Do you hack, Simon?" Rita asks, not expecting an answer but he replies straight away "Of course I do but only for good reasons. I don't do anything bad."

"Okay." says Rita quickly, not wishing to offend him. "I didn't think you would." Then she has another question.

"So a keylogger might get in through, say, a game. Is there another way to hack?"

"Well, yes. You have heard of the Trojan Horse?"

Rita agrees she is familiar with the story of the giant wooden horse the Greeks used to get inside the walls of Troy but wonders what point Simon is making.

"Well, there are codes – sometimes called viruses but they are not really that - which act like the Trojan Horse. As the computer user, you let them in, then they do bad things, maybe send information to the hacker, maybe destroy parts of your software, or email your friends to say you are in trouble when you are not."

"So how does a user let the code in?" Rita asks next.

"Most usually through social networking. For example, it might be part of an email attachment. That's why you should not open anything you are not sure of."

"What use do people make of it if they gain access to computers?" Rita wants to know.

"They might want your bank details or personal information. Email addresses are very useful to hackers so they can carry out more fraud. Or they might publish personal details if they are doing it for a political reason, or they might sell the information. You remember that Sony PlayStation had a security problem in 2011 when some of their data was stolen? People are working all the time to try to make sure things like that don't happen. Good hackers have to outwit bad ones!" Simon exclaims.

"Do you think the police would be able to tell if a computer has been hacked?" Rita asks Simon as she stands on the bridge in the park looking over the reed-fringed lake.

"If they have computer people who are good, like me!" he says.

"And what is the punishment for hacking?" Rita wants to know.

"Under our law you can be imprisoned for up to 10 years for impairing a computer." Simon tells her. "But the Government will probably try to change that. I think they want a longer sentence where national security is put at risk. And of course if you hack a United States computer they can extradite you, so then you would face penalties under their law."

"Is it just individuals who do it?" Rita asks him, thinking of geeks alone in their bedrooms.

"Not just them." Simon says, "There are organisations – 'hacktivists' they call themselves - who hack together for a purpose. There are groups you may have heard of, like Anonymous and Lulzsec."

"But you don't belong to any of them?" Rita is worried for Simon now.

"No. I just follow what they are doing sometimes." he reassures her. "Some hackers boast about what they are doing in chat rooms." he adds.

Rita thanks Simon and says she will call him again if she needs more information. She thinks she would like Simon to look at Mr Halliwell's computer, but she knows that is not possible. She watches the ducks diving under the rippling water and appearing again, shaking their heads as if looking for something they cannot find.

* * *

Thursday, 24th October 2013 7pm

Rita has returned to Aunty Gee's despondently and now they are on their way together to BAPS Shri Swaminarayan Mandir, Neasden Temple, weighed down with offerings of fruit and flowers. Rita is also weighed down with worry for her brother whom, as Mr Beresford warned her, the police have charged with the murder of Mervyn Halliwell. The 'breaking news' on the red strips which convey information beneath the news screens simply says "A 20 year old man has been charged. He will appear before magistrates tomorrow."

"Poor Mohal!" says Aunty Gee "What a terrible thing! And your poor parents!" Priya has phoned to express her concern and to find out about Rita's day. There was not much to say, so for once they did not speak for long.Priya could detect dejection in her friend's voice. "Good luck for the court tomorrow!" was all she could think of to say.

Rita and Aunty Gee enter with others through the Haveli, a wooden structure next to the stone temple, and walk up the wheelchair ramp as that is easier for her aunt than the steep steps. The temple which rises above the closely packed houses in this area of north London dwarfs them and looks like a large elaborate grey sandcastle, with flags flying from the many domed construction. The Haveli has a prayer centre, gymnasium and other facilities. Inside the temple itself there are many intricately carved pillars maintaining a decorated ceiling and the gods are bathed in golden light. Aunty Gee has put on her best purple sari and Rita wears the cream shalwar kameez which her mother made her pack; they are pleased to be well turned out as are many others, and they walk slowly round the vast building looking at the marble and wood carvings, then sit quietly and meditate under the dome. Rita feels some feelings of calm returning to her and a renewed desire to do whatever she can to help her brother. They see various friends of Aunty Gee as they stare at the beauty around them and soak in the peace of the place, but of course they cannot discuss what is most on their mind as that would betray Mohal's involvement.

Leaving the temple the two women notice the intricately laid out gardens surrounding the temple building and resolve to return to enjoy the gardens fully. "Better in the spring I think." says Aunty Gee. They take a taxi back to her house where she orders a take away for them while Rita makes last minute arrangements on the telephone with Mr Beresford about where to meet at court the following day.

Chapter

6

"People must not do things for fun. We are not here for fun. There is no reference to fun in any Act of Parliament."

A.P. Herbert

Friday, 25th October 2013 9am

I suppose I could have killed myself rather than you, but that would have been giving in to you Mr Halliwell, wouldn't it? And what about your glittering career? Would you have continued onward and upward? Would you have made Secretary of State? Were you too valuable to your Prime Minister to be sacked? Maybe you would have become PM yourself or, more likely, got a peerage so you can lord it (literally) over the rest of us in your robes and ermine. I bet your wife would like to have been Lady Halliwell (Of where I wonder? Somewhere local? Oakham? Empingham has a ring to it? I doubt you would have chosen Highfields or Rushey Mead, not posh enough.) But it's academic now, you've gone to the debating chamber in the sky, if it exists. Better luck next time, but mind how you behave, your karma will find you out.

What about me? I'm not worried about myself. Your death was justified.I will plead not guilty of course, so I can expose you at my trial. You deserved it for what you did to me, and God knows how many others, I will be vindicated.

* * *

Friday, 25th October 2013 10am

"Miss Patel." Tim Beresford, finds Rita in the melee that is the crowd of family, friends and supporters of accused and victims, together with the traffic offenders, fine defaulters and people who have not paid for their television licences, in the magistrates court that day. As well as lawyers greeting their clients in any quiet corner they can find, there are social workers, probation officers, and translators, all trying to find the people they are here to serve, crossing and recrossing the floor like agitated City workers on a busy stock exchange floor, and these are interspersed with uniformed people - police and prison officers acknowledging each other and the court staff, as they come and go.

The man standing at the reception desk had been very helpful when Rita arrived.

"Mr Beresford? Yes, we know him. He's been here before. Just you wait over there and he'll find you."

"Now then." Mr Beresford opens his large blue notebook as he arrives and he balances this on his knee as he sits next to Rita on a bench "The police have spoken to me and your brother's been examined by a doctor to check he is ok to plead. I gather your parents are coming back from abroad tomorrow?" Rita confirms that since she had met with Mr Beresford the previous day her parents have contacted her to say that they will be on a flight out of India the next day, and that her uncle is coming to the court for moral support.

"Very well." Mr Beresford says, "Mohal is likely to be remanded in custody while the police and CPS prepare for the trial. We can try for bail but I'm not hopeful. There's no clear motive, of course. The police don't think your brother represents a risk to anyone, the Leicester police have been helpful about that, but they are concerned he may abscond before his trial."

"Abscond?" Rita is surprised.

"Yes. They would have egg on their face if he skipped the country before his trial. So even if we can get bail for him - and I stress that's not likely - they will want him to report to the police station."

"Which police station?" Rita asks, wondering how Mohal will manage in London, alone with nothing to do but brood on his fate.

"We can influence that. I'm guessing it would be better all round if he was at your parents' house - his home - and reported to the Leicester police station?" Tim Beresford speculates.

Rita can see this is a better idea and agrees.

"Well, it's not certain he will get bail, but we can ask, so fingers crossed and chin up. Let's go in." Mr Beresford leads the way.

It is the first time that Rita has been inside a court room. It feels very impersonal she thinks, like an office with no windows or pictures, just plain light wood panelling all round the walls on which the spotlights above shine a yellow glow, and a coat of arms facing her as she sits, as directed by Mr Beresford, on a bench at the back of the room. The place is stark and business-like, contrasting, in Rita's mind, with the high domed finely decorated temple she had visited the day before. There are rows of seats, like in a theatre, a desk in the middle where one of the court officials sits, and a raised platform facing them. Tim Beresford goes to sit at the front with the other legal representatives. People are talking in hushed tones as if it were a religious building and this effect is enhanced when the judge enters, silence descends, everyone is told to stand up ("All rise!") and the lawyers, who are several rows in front of Rita, bow their heads to the District Judge who reciprocates before they all sit down.

From her vantage point, Rita can see the court has an upper floor. Various people are seated in the gallery to watch proceedings. Most look bored and as if this is a place they visit often. To the left of them, as Rita scans across, is a group of half a dozen individuals with note books open and phones whose screens they consult frequently while often checking their watches, the opposite of the indolent spectators next to them. These must be reporters from the press, Rita concludes. She had noticed a TV van on the road outside near the court, a raised dish on the roof making it look like something from outer space. So there was a lot of press interest even in this small hearing, she notes; the murder of an MP was big news and there was precious little they could report. The pieces she had seen on TV and online had consisted of 10% information and 90% speculation with wild theories being advanced connected with Mr Halliwell's financial affairs, enemies he made as a councillor before his election to Parliament, his opposition to certain Syrian charities and similar fanciful ideas. After a while she had stopped looking at them.

The judge is a kindly looking woman, probably in her fifties Rita thinks, with spectacles which she wears on a chain round her neck when she is not using them. When she puts the glasses on to read from her papers, Rita notices how far down her nose they perch, she almost needs an extension to her nose. This thought makes Rita want to laugh, which would be most inappropriate; it must be her nervousness on her brother's behalf, she thinks.

"Hi Rita." a voice whispers to her left as her uncle, Bandhu, Jaina's husband, slips into the seat next to her just as the judge is talking to one of the lawyers at the front. The guilty pleas are dealt with first and Rita watches as an array of people – all men - appear in the glass fronted box to the side of the court, like contestants in a television game show. They plead guilty to drink driving, taking a car without consent (Rita learns the acronym for this is 'TWOC' which can also be used as a verb apparently), and stealing alcohol from a supermarket. The cases are adjourned so the offenders can talk to probation officers and recommendations can be made for sentencing. The motley crew of guilty individuals melts away and suddenly Mohal appears instead.

Seeing her brother standing there, stranded behind the glass panel, like a volunteer in a magic show, Rita gasps. He looks like he has shrunk. Her usually proud brother, who stands several inches above his sister, holds his head down and his shoulders are curved inwards. Rita is shocked to see he has the start of a beard, which, together with the grey track suit he is wearing, adds to his sorrowful appearance. The two words he speaks when asked ("Not guilty") emerge uneasily from a dry mouth. After this statement, Mohal is allowed to sit.

The trial will be at the Crown Court, the judge says, which is as Mr Beresford had told Rita; in view of the seriousness of the crime and the not guilty plea, a trial would need to take place before a jury. Rita recalls that juries – trial by a committee of 12 men – was a Danish concept introduced to England by the Vikings and developed into a system in the 12th century under Henry II. At that time juries would investigate as well as determine the outcome. Of course, she thinks, jury trial is a right in Article 39 of Magna Carta and she recalls a translation she has read –

"No freeman shall be captured or imprisoned or disseised of his freehold, or of his liberties, or of his free customs, or be outlawed or exiled or in any way destroyed, nor will we proceed against him by force or proceed against him by arms, but by the lawful judgment of his peers or by the law of the land."

The tiny figure of the female lawyer for the CPS (Crown Prosecution Service, as Mr Beresford explained to Rita yesterday) tells the magistrate that Mr Mohal Patel, as she calls him, has been in police custody since Tuesday and there is concern that if released on bail he may abscond while inquiries continue. Mr Beresford stands as the lady lawyer sits down – they are like clockwork figures, Rita thinks, bobbing up and down. Mr Beresford says the evidence so far is circumstantial and there is an unfortunate absence of CCTV material for the time and place in question. He draws the judge's attention to material from the Leicester police and community leaders from the temple stating Mohal has never been in trouble and is thought to be from a good caring family. Tim Beresford tells the judge that Mr Patel's parents are currently on their way back from visiting relatives in India but that his uncle has agreed to provide bail assurances and at this Rita looks sideways at Bandhu, gratefully. Mr Beresford says the Metropolitan Police do not consider Mr Patel a risk to others ('Mohal a risk to anyone? How could they think that?' Rita thinks) but he understands the authorities are concerned that if released he may seek to leave the country (Rita is indignant on her brother's behalf at this). The woman lawyer rises to nod to confirm this information and then for once both lawyers are standing while the judge thinks out loud, waving her spectacles in the air as if to demonstrate a point.

"So Miss Chen you're not opposing bail as such?" the CPS lawyer indicates agreement, "I think we can address the flight risk Mr Beresford, don't you?" the judge says and he nods.

"I do, Madam" he says "Mr Patel is willing to surrender his passport and to report to the police station every day. He would prefer, if the police concur, to reside at the parental home, in Leicester. You and the police officers concerned have his parents' address, Madam." he says.

"Yes, Mr Beresford.I can see the sense in what you say." the judge agrees. "And it seems to me the police may need a quite a bit of time to gather more evidence, Miss Chen?" The woman lawyer nods.

"Have you anything to say?" the judge asks her, "What do your clients think about Mr Patel residing in Leicester? Are you still concerned about a flight risk if he gives up his passport?"

"Madam." Miss Chen responds, having spoken swiftly to a young woman sitting behind her who looks not much older than Rita. "The police investigations into this terrible crime are still at an early stage and there is much evidence to be confirmed as you have mentioned so my clients would not press for Mr Patel to held in custody especially in view of his youth and the fact that there is no suggestion as yet that this was anything but the personal act of an individual. But my clients are concerned at the flight risk."

'Oh no' thinks Rita 'Maybe they won't let Mohal come home after all! What will her parents say?' She and Bandhu exchange apprehensive looks. The thought of Mohal in prison is more than she can bear, and coming to London to see him would be very difficult for everyone.

"So we would be willing for Mr Patel to be subject to a curfew order." Miss Chen continues.

"Yes, Miss Chen." says the judge taking her glasses off her nose so they dangle against her chest. She leans forward to confer briefly with the court official in front of her.

"Very well." the judge says, leaning back in her chair "This is what I'm going to do. Bail will be posted with the court office by 4pm today. Mr Patel will travel under police escort to Leicester. He will surrender his passport to the police there and report to the station there every day at 11am. He will also be subject to a curfew enforced through electronic tagging. He is to refrain from making any telephone calls or using the internet. The curfew remains in force from 9pm to 9am. Reporting restrictions are not lifted." She speaks this last sentence slowly and looks up to the press in the gallery deliberately.

"Have you anything to say Mr Beresford?" the judge asks.

Rita watches Mohal's lawyer go over to the glass box and speak to her brother through a window. Mr Beresford nods and returns to his place.

"Yes, Madam. My client confirms he will cooperate with those arrangements. He will need to notify his University as to where he is staying" ('Oh dear' thinks Rita, 'Whatever will they think?').

"I expect you will make them aware of the situation." the judge says dryly. "And I expect they will be able to help Mr Patel in his predicament pending his trial."

Mr Beresford turns to nod to Rita and Bandhu as Mohal disappears below ground ('It is rather like a conjuring trick' Rita thinks). At least she can tell her parents that Mohal is coming home!

* * *

Friday, 25th October 2013 2pm

Rita returns home to Leicester that afternoon, driven by Bandhu in his Toyota Prius. The M1 is busy and slow owing to the constant rain from the storms which the forecasters had been excited about all week; this is causing plumes of spray to rise up across the lanes whenever a lorry or bus goes by, obscuring everyone's view; not surprisingly, there has been an accident at Newport Pagnel and another is highlighted on the overhead gantry as having occurred at junction 20. When Rita and her uncle finally draw up outside Rita's parents' house in Elm Drive it feels like they have been on the road for days not just the 3 hours which the 100 mile journey has taken. Since the traffic was moving so slowly in the wet conditions – the advisory limit of 40mph was mocking them as they crawled along at 15mph at most - they had stopped at the Northampton services to fortify themselves with tea.

The shock of the last few hours was beginning to wear off as she sipped her tea and Rita's brain was starting to race again. How could the police think Mohal was guilty? How could she help him? One thing she had learned from what Mr Beresford told the magistrate, and from questioning him afterwards, was that the CCTV in Portcullis House, which would surely have shown the killer entering and leaving Mr Halliwell's office, was not working at the crucial time. There was no record of who had visited the office between 11.45 and 2.45. In the absence of any video evidence, Rita wrestled with ideas as to how Mohal could prove he was not involved in the death.

They did not pick up petrol at the services ("The Prius is very economical and I won't pay motorway prices if I can help it." says Bandhu.) They had rejoined the vehicles moving at funereal pace and their slow progress had continued until past Hinckley when the sky cleared for a while, the pace picked up, and they were able to overtake and manoeuvre across lanes with other cars doing the same, Bandhu taking extra care on the wet surface. Her uncle made full use of all the lanes as if to make a point. Rita tried to understand what he was doing, how he knew when it was safe to pull out and when to pull into the left, but it was pretty hard to discern. She realised, however, that you had to watch carefully for other drivers acting unpredictably. There was a car which suddenly slowed down after it had overtaken them,for example, and another which shot by them on the left unexpectedly.

They are surprised to find when they get out of the car at Rita's house that Mohal is already inside, having been dropped off by the police to whom he has given his passport. He has been told to stay indoors and wait for G4S to come with the tagging equipment. Mohal makes a chastened figure, almost hollowed out by his nights in the police cells. His unshaven appearance gives his jaw an unfamiliar, more square shape and accentuates the hollowness of his eyes. His hair has been dampened down but not combed in his accustomed style. In the track suit the police have given him, suitably grey in colour, his shoulders sag, he seems almost to limp, his legs look like they may buckle at any time. His rolled-up sleeves reveal some writing on his right arm which Rita cannot quite make out. Has her brother had a tattoo since she last saw him?

"Cheese on toast!" says Rita, after they have hugged briefly, anything too enthusiastic and Mohal looks like he might break. She knows this is one of her brother's favourite things to eat. "I'll bring it through to the living room" another treat as their mother, Padma, insists they eat in the large breakfast kitchen to keep crumbs out of the rest of the house.

"That would be great." joins in Bandhu with a falsely jolly tone, copying Rita's lead and realising that they need to do what they can to lift Mohal's mood.

"Then you can tell us all about it." Bandhu adds "And we can see what we can do." adds Rita.

Mohal lifts his head at that, like an animal listening out for a familiar cry. It is as if he were using the sound of Rita's voice to reorient himself, to help him find a direction of travel instead of the helplessness into which he seems to have slumped.

Chapter

7

> *"Politics is like waking up in the morning. You never know whose head you will find on the pillow."*
> Winston Churchill

Friday, 25th October 2013 5pm

People did complain, you know! After what happened to me I checked it out. If you knew where to look online there were several stories circulating. Of how people said he went too far. But nobody listened. Nobody wanted to listen. "We're a political party not a police force" "MPs lead busy pressured lives." "Everyone drinks too much sometimes." And so on. He didn't get investigated in the past, he got promoted! And I guess the higher you climb the harder it is for the powers that be to admit they made a mistake. Friends in high places have friends in high places. You scratch my back and I'll scratch yours. How many people really knew? Were they covering up deliberately? Did they do it to protect themselves or him? Was it power, or influence, or fear that bought the ring of silence around him? Well the noise will be deafening soon.

* * *

Friday, 25th October 2013 6pm

From the next room, as she boils the kettle and toasts the bread in the kitchen, Rita can hear Bandhu ask Mohal when the tagging people will come. Mohal admits "They don't know exactly. They said they'd be here before nine tonight, when the curfew starts." Then Bandhu's phone rings and he steps into the hall to speak in quiet tones to his wife, Jaina,

78

who has just finished her work as a school secretary for the day and is home looking after their twin daughters, Shreya and Shona.

"Yes, I am at Padma's with Rita. Mohal is here. Out on bail. He won't be able to leave the house at night." He does not elaborate. "See you all later." Rita takes the tray of food into the living room and Bandhu helps her carry the mugs of camomile tea.

"Thanks, Rita." She has never known her brother so appreciative. "When do Mum and Dad get back?" Mohal says next, his voice sounding weak. "I feel bad about spoiling their holiday."

"It's not your fault." says Rita quickly. "And of course they wanted to come back and help you. They just had trouble getting a flight. It's a busy time. It'll be some time tomorrow morning."

Mohal quickly devours a piece of the cheese on toast and helps himself to another. Bandhu takes a piece and Rita takes a bite out of hers saying "Eat as much as you like, I can make some more."

After more munching, Bandhu can bear it no longer.

"Now you have to tell us what happened." he says.

"We know a bit from Mr Beresford and Inspector Bridge," Rita adds, "But none of it makes sense."

"It doesn't make sense to me either, sis," Mohal mutters, "It's proper mental." After a bit more chewing he continues.

"I can't believe I can't contact my friends, I can't use my phone, I can't go on Facebook or YouTube, I can't tell anyone I'm stuck here while they make up their case against me!"

"Make up the case?" Rita asks immediately.

"What do you mean?" asks their uncle.

"Well, you know. Look guys," Mohal appeals to both, his hands stretched out imploringly, "I didn't do it, okay, you have to believe me?"

"Of course we do." Rita says and Bandhu nods. Rita leans

forward and touches her brother's arm, which is shaking.

"Have some more tea." says Bandhu, going into the kitchen although he is reluctant to miss any of Mohal's story. Mohal rises to look out at the garden, the garden he has largely ignored or derided in the past and which now he will be forbidden from entering for several hours a day; never did it look more appealing. All those years he had despised his father's efforts at creating a decked area and planting beds and how much he would give now to be able to walk among those flowers whenever he wants.

He sits down, a bit more composed, as Bandhu returns with more tea for them all. "I just don't see how it all points to me unless someone's planted evidence, or is playing games… And now they have my fingerprints and my DNA who knows what they could fabricate – you know the UK has the biggest DNA database in Europe?" he goes on. Rita thinks Mohal has had too long on his own to think about this. Fanciful theories about being framed would not help him.

"Tell us." says Bandhu. "You found the body, yes?"

"It was horrible." Mohal says.

Rita, who has opened her iPad to make notes, tries to impose some order on Mohal's tale. "So this was Tuesday lunchtime?"

"Yeah, I guess. Yeah. He has had an office in Portcullis House – PCH we call it for short – which is that building near the Houses of Parliament. Mr Halliwell had a meeting booked – it was in the diary; a constituent was coming to his office at 2.15pm. We call those meetings surgeries. Well, I got to his office not long after 1.45, I found it was locked which usually meant he wasn't there."

"You have a key?" Rita asks her brother.

"Well, yeah. The police made a big deal of it. So I opened."

"Unlocked?" Rita chips in.

"Yeah. I unlocked the office door and went in. Mr Halliwell was there at the meeting table, which surprised me, his back was towards me." Mohal describes the scene as if he's done so several times before. Impossible to know whether what he is recalling is what he saw or what he has been repeating so many times it has become so, Rita thinks.

"I said, I dunno, something lame like 'Hello Mr Halliwell, shall I stay for the meeting?', then I went round the table to face him since he didn't move. I suppose... I don't think I registered that he hadn't moved, then I saw his face was very still. He was literally just sitting there, leaning against the wall, his arms on the table. So then I thought maybe he wasn't well, was having a stroke or something, I don't know. So I went to his side of the table and I said, 'Are you all right?' Or something like that and I touched him on the shoulder and then I realised… I realised."

Mohal puts his hands over his face as if to blot out what he saw.

"And then I could see blood, blood seeping through his jacket at the back and I looked and there was blood coming through his shirt and my hands had blood on them and I... I panicked… I didn't know what to do... I ran ...I ran out of the office and down the stairs... I didn't use the lift, I don't know why… I don't know what I was thinking… I carried on running and went out of the side of the building. I needed air, fresh air. I needed to be somewhere, anywhere, else, but there… and then I felt sick so – I know it sounds mad - I crossed the road, I don't know how, the traffic is really bad, I think I could hear cars honking their horns at me... I crossed the road, went to the bridge, I looked over and heaved but I couldn't actually be sick, it was just a dry heave, you know?" he looks to his uncle and sister for understanding.

"And then I turned to go back to the building - to PCH - I thought I needed to tell someone, no one else should walk in on that sight; and as I walked towards it the security guards and a police officer came out towards me and stopped the traffic. We met on the pedestrian island between the lanes and I said, I dunno; "Mr Halliwell's dead." or something like that and they saw the blood on my hands and they got me down on the pavement and shouted at me "Have you got any weapons, have you hurt Mr Halliwell?"

(Rita recalls the scene from the news programmes and online services which had carried mobile phone footage of a man (her brother) lying on the ground with his arms pinned behind him and two hefty men looming over him, one with a submachine gun in his hand. It was very scaring to watch never mind to be the subject of.)

"And there were police arriving all the time and sirens blaring and alarms going off."

(Rita knows they closed down Portcullis House and the Houses of Parliament for several hours, democracy was interrupted in case there was a national emergency.)

"And all their radios were buzzing with messages and they asked me my name and handcuffed me and put me in a van – this was all on Victoria Embankment - and... and... I was so scared... you hear all the time about black men being fitted up and beaten up by the police, guilty until proved innocent." Mohal is close to tears by now as he tells his story and rubs at his eyes.

"Take it easy." says Bandhu, "There's no rush."

The telephone in the living room rings and all three jump, showing how Mohal's story has affected them. Rita picks up the handset on the coffee table. It is her parents.

"Hi Mum, yes he's home, Yes, he's fine." Mohal and Bandhu can hear her say.

"No, he can't come to the phone, he's not supposed to use it, it's part of his curfew terms".

Mohal nods to confirm as Rita looks at him. There is a lot of talking at the other end and Rita is confronted with a choice between displeasing Her Majesty's court and law enforcement officers or displeasing her mother; she opts for the former. Rita puts her hand over the mouthpiece.

"She won't take no for an answer. Surely no one will know? If you just tell her you're okay?" she pleads and holds the phone out to her brother who reluctantly takes it and says quickly "Hi Mum, I'm fine. I'm here. I'm sorry for the trouble I've caused." and he hands the phone back to Rita.

"Okay now?" Rita asks her mother. "What time are you due back tomorrow?" then she says "Bandhu can stay tonight. It's one of the bail conditions that Mohal has an adult in the house with him." When there is a pause in the talking at the India end of the conversation Rita gets in "Okay Mum. Good flight. See you soon." And Rita hangs up.

"Is Mum mad at me?" Mohal wants to know, looking at Rita imploringly.

"Not really," Rita tries to reassure him. She doesn't tell her brother that their parents have seen his arrest on the internet; they and the relatives they are visiting are shocked and worried.

"She's concerned, of course, and wants to know you are ok. The parents think it must be all a misunderstanding, which it is, isn't it?" Rita prompts Mohal to continue his story.

"Of course," says Mohal, "but I don't understand how they thought they could charge me; the evidence, it can't be real, since I didn't do it." he trails off, face puzzled.

"So," says Rita looking at her notes, "He was stabbed?"

"Yeah, I gather. That's what the police said. Where's the knife? What did you do with the knife Mohal?" He is reliving his interrogation.

"No knife in the room then?" Rita checks.

"So they said. They said I must have run across the road to throw away the knife in the Thames."

"So they haven't found it at all?" his sister asks.

"Nope." Mohal shakes his head in confirmation.

"And your key?" Rita asks.

"Was still on me, in my jacket pocket. I think I took it out, unlocked the door, and put it back in my pocket after I'd unlocked it. I s'pose. I didn't think about it while I was doing it. It was automatic." Mohal explains.

"So they found you with a key, blooded hands, and no knife." Bandhu summarises,

"Yeah, but I mean if I'd done it, and if I'd thrown the knife away, why would I walk back towards PCH, why wouldn't I keep running? Why wouldn't I get away?" Mohal wrings his hands.

"It's okay." says Bandhu soothingly, "We believe you Mohal. We need to understand why the police don't." He looks across to Rita for confirmation.

"Mr Beresford." says Mohal, as if remembering, "I'm supposed to go and see him tomorrow, he'll contact a barrister for me. I'll have to keep going over it, over and over…" he hangs his head as if it's all a lot of effort.

"There must be more." says Rita "More than you finding the body and running off." she clarifies.

"Oh yeah." says Mohal as Bandhu's eyes widen, "There is." ('What more could there be?' thinks Rita.)

"There's been a bit of a hate campaign against Mr Halliwell. I heard about it because his diary secretary, Camilla, told us, me and Sebastian. I mean, Mr Halliwell's political adviser."

"What hate campaign?" Rita asks.

"There was nothing in the news about it." Bandhu adds.

"No, it was kept out of the press. The police advised them to. Thought it might be easier to catch the guy and anyway better not to let him have the satisfaction of publicity." Mohal explains.

"So what happened?" Bandhu again.

"His car got scratched, when it was right outside his house in Oakham. Someone scratched the word 'DIE' on the side."

"When was this?" Rita asks, keen to see if Mohal has an alibi.

"Well, that's the bad thing." Mohal says, "It was not long after I'd started with Mr Halliwell. It was the day he sent me to fetch some papers from his house. When they were in London having the debate on Syria."

"Okay." says Rita, not convinced that this is conclusive against her brother, "And tools?"

Mohal laughs a sort of barking laugh, "Well I've got the screwdrivers in the boot of my car, haven't I? From trying to fix the washing machine at the student house."

"Where is your car?" Bandhu asks, having just thought about it. Rita knows the answer and explains. It had been outside the house in Neasden. Aunty Gee had described to her how the police had arrived with a low loader and taken it away. She said that Mohal's little Peugeot had made a sad and lonely sight as it was carried in stately fashion to the end of the road and disappeared round the corner to some police forensic lab where, no doubt, Rita now realises, they are testing the screwdrivers for traces of paint from Mr Halliwell's car.

"Have the police taken anything else?" Mohal suddenly asks as if the two realities of the police station and home had begun to merge together, like two eyes coming into focus to make one picture.

"Oh they had a good search." Rita informs him, "Of your room at Neasden and the house here, mainly your room, and I expect they've been to the student house too."

"I'll have to ask Ravi." Mohal says automatically, referring to one of his housemates, then, "Oh no, I forgot, I'm not allowed. Can you speak to them, Rita?" he asks, "Apologise for me," he adds.

"Of course," says Rita, glad to be useful, and makes another note.

"So far it's all circumstantial." she points out to Mohal, "And I understand the CCTV outside Mr Halliwell's office was not working at the crucial time so that's no help. Is there anything else?"

"There's the paint," says Mohal, but before he can explain

further the door bell rings.

The next hour is taken up with getting the tagging equipment installed to the satisfaction of the G4S contractor. He is the silent type, only communicating when he needs to explain how the system works or requires a signature. Rita thinks maybe that's what you learn on this job. You'd be going to the homes of all kinds of people, guilty, innocent, habitual criminals and people having their first brush with the law. The one thing they would all have in common, Rita guesses, is resentment; they would not welcome the erosion of their freedom that the tagging equipment represents and if you were fitting it you probably learnt to say as little as possible and get quickly. It wasn't an occasion for polite small talk, Rita can see that.

The man has a black box, about the size of a radio or CD player, which has a phone attached. He installs this on the bookcase in the living room; anyone visiting them and noticing it would think it was another phone, Rita thinks, trying to see how things will look from her mother's perspective when she arrives back. Then he fits a tag on Mohal's right leg, at the ankle. It is like a metal bracelet. The man makes a joke – "Just checking your leg's real." he says "We've been caught out with artificial ones before now."

Then Mohal walks about the house, going into all the rooms, so the man can calibrate the tagging machine. "You don't smoke?" he asks. Mohal confirms. "If you did I'd give you a bit of the garden at the back," the man says, "but there's no need." Rita shrugs. Mohal would have been better off if he did smoke! She thinks.

The man rings his office on the phone and confirms the hours of the curfew, "9pm to 9am" he says. He explains to them all that if Mohal is not in the house between those hours the alarm will be raised. Also, that they may be called at any time on the phone on the tagging machine and they must answer it ('Bit like Big Brother', Rita thinks,' but with serious consequences'). With that, the man leaves, driving away in his anonymous black Ford Focus. The tagging has depressed Mohal's spirits. He looks dejected again and his shoulders are slumping.

"Why not take a shower?" Rita suggests. "You can wash with the tag on?" she checks suddenly.

"Oh yeah, the bloke said. It's waterproof. Well, it'd have to be." Mohal replies.

So Mohal goes upstairs to shower and change out of the police tracksuit. Rita finds a vegetable curry which Padma has left in the freezer and heats it up with some naan bread, while Bandhu watches the news on television. The shocking murder of an MP at Portcullis House where he was supposed to be meeting a constituent has slipped from the first news item and features 3rd or 4th. Rita is glad Mohal is still out of the room when the item comes on.

"A man has appeared in court today in connection with the murder of Mervyn Halliwell, the Minister who was stabbed to death on Tuesday. The man, aged 20, was released on bail and is subject to curfew conditions. He is required to report to the police on a daily basis while inquiries continue. For security purposes reporting restrictions apply and we are not allowed to give any details of the man who has been charged."

'Thank goodness' thinks Rita the last thing her parents need is to come home to a road full of reporters. But how long before the news gets out? The family, the Neasden relatives, Mohal's University friends, all know about Mohal. Any one of them could give him away however inadvertently. Rita thinks she had better keep any eye on Twitter and Facebook in case there is speculation linked to Mohal.

Just as she thinks this, her brother walks into the kitchen, looking better for being in his own clothes – he has put on a rugby shirt over some jeans. The right sleeve of the Leicester Tigers shirt is rolled up and Rita can see better the writing on

Mohal's arm which she caught sight of in court. 'Has he had a tattoo since he's been in London?' she wonders.

"Feeling better?" she asks and as he nods she cannot help adding, "What's that?" indicating his arm.

"Oh" Mohal is rather embarrassed and starts to roll down his sleeve. "An imam came to see me in the police cells."

"An imam?" Rita cannot help looking astonished. "Why on earth?"

"Well, he's a chaplain for them. The police like to have one on hand, you know, in case they have any Muslims in custody. It saves rows about food and prayers and so on."

"If you say so." Rita is not convinced. "But the writing?" Now she has looked closer she can see the writing is not in English. It's in Arabic.

"The imam told me not to worry. If I am innocent – which I am – he said his God would protect me. I was pretty scared Rita, you've no idea." Mohal clenches his fists and sinks the top of his body down on his arms onto the kitchen counter as he speaks, the memory of his questioning returning vividly.

"He wrote on my arm, it must be strong ink as it hasn't washed off, it says 'In the remembrance of God do hearts find ease.' It's from the Qur'an."

"I guessed that much." says Rita still not impressed. Why should Mohal think about the Muslim God?

"The Qur'an speaks of remembrance of God as a way for believers to strengthen their faith, purify their hearts and find peace in times of turmoil. Glorifying and praising God helps calm the soul." her brother goes on to Rita's surprise.

"You seem to have remembered a lot about what he said." Rita says suspiciously, suddenly recalling one of Inspector Bridge's questions, ("Has Mohal been to a mosque? Has he expressed any interest in Islam?") Thank goodness she knew nothing about this when she answered emphatically in the negative. And what would her father think if he knew Mohal had even been entertaining such thoughts, never mind getting comfort from an imam? Something else she needs to keep from her parents if she can, Rita thinks.

"I have looked into a bit actually." Her brother looks up from the kitchen counter shyly, "From an academic point of view I mean." he adds hastily. "I just wanted to know more, what people see in it. So I already knew some of the stuff he was saying. And he wasn't heavy about it or anything. He was genuinely trying to put my mind at ease."

"Doesn't change the fact you're not a Muslim!" Rita finds it hard not to shout at her brother, only the memory of his sad figure in the dock earlier stops her. "You shouldn't play with these ideas! It can get you into trouble!" she hisses at him.

* * *

Friday 25th October 2013 8.30pm

Rita and Bandhu allow Mohal to relax over supper before asking him to take up the story about the paint. So it is gone 8.30pm and close to the start of the curfew period when Mohal explains. He tells them that a month after the incident with the car Mr Halliwell had come back to his house in Oakham to find a message in large white letters painted in the driveway, the message said 'DIE MERVYN'.

"A month later?" Rita checks. "Yes", says Mohal looking bewildered again, "That's the problem. It was that Sunday, the day we all went for a walk round the reservoir."

Rita thinks back. She had been in the car on the journey to Rutland Water with her parents and Nayan. Mohal had been to see a friend in Uppingham – someone he had been at school with - and drove himself. The reservoir was created in the 1970s to meet the needs of expanding populations in places like Peterborough. Filled with water from the rivers Welland and Nene, and the largest man made lake in Western

Europe, it made an ideal place for a family stroll and picnic, which is what they enjoyed that day, although the sky and the water had been an ominous navy colour for some of the time, Rita recalled. There were nature reserves all around the reservoir so there were lots of birds to see; the water was used for numerous activities and it was fun to watch the rowers and paddlers and wind surfers. Other people were cycling round the 25 mile perimeter, ideal because the terrain was so flat, so they had to keep a look out for bikes. Normanton Church rose above the water, its floor level having been raised and its masonry damp-proofed; the church houses a museum showing the history of the reservoir, which Rita had visited. Nether Hambleton – know as the 'lost village' - lies under Rutland Water and was once a large medieval settlement, Rita had learned. Recalling the fun day out they had all enjoyed, it seems a long way from the troubled times they are now in, Rita thinks.

"Well, Mr Beresford needs to find the exact time the damage was done." Rita offers what comfort she can, "Because we know when you left Ned's." this was Mohal's friend "And when you met us. And after that we were all together. You drove back with Nayan." she recalls.

"Yeah." Mohal does not appear to be cheered by this analysis. "They reckon it was about 2 o'clock. Mr Halliwell went for a walk and to a pub and found the damage when he got back about 3pm. I left Ned at 1.30 and met you at 2.30 or so?"

"More like 2.45." Rita says factually but not helpfully.

"So according to the feds," Bandhu winces at the term, "Sorry." Mohal corrects himself "The police. I had time to pop to Oakham and paint the message." (Rita thinks it explains why the police took away Jahi's white paint. More work for their forensic lab, assuming there was any paint to compare it with.)

"There's more. It was bad luck really that we painted

the study that night. So when I saw Sebastian the next day he pointed out I had white flakes in my hair. He said was I getting prematurely old?" Rita recalls the scene in the study. Father and son had managed to make a lot of mess in a small space and despite taking showers afterwards both had paint speckles in their hair. Mohal gathered that Sebastian's observation had been passed on to Camilla, Mr Halliwell's diary secretary, and she had passed it on to the police.

"But no one saw who did it? The paint or the scratch on the car?" Rita asks.

"Not that they told me..." Mohal confirms, "They just seem determined to say it was me. They are just building up the evidence so it fits me." he says disconsolately.

"And Tuesday." Rita checks, "If Mr Halliwell was stabbed before you arrived, where were you?"

"Where was I?" Mohal repeats, zombie-like.

"Yes, Mohal." Rita knows when her brother is stalling.

"I was at lunch." he offers, not elaborating.

"Well, where?" Rita prompts. "Can someone vouch for you?"

"No." Mohal is quick to answer. "No I was alone. In the park and then Victoria Street. No one saw me."

There is something in Mohal's face which makes Rita think he is not telling the truth, or the whole truth, but she decides not to challenge him that evening. He's clearly had enough.

"Don't worry old chap." Bandhu reassures "We'll talk to the lawyers tomorrow and find out how to get you out of this. They can't seriously press ahead with so little actual evidence." But as he speaks he looks across at Rita and shakes his head. How are they to prove Mohal is innocent?

Chapter

8

"He is asked to stand, he wants to sit, he is expected to lie."

Winston Churchill,
definition of a Parliamentary candidate

Saturday, 26th October 2013 (morning)

Everyone in Elm Drive had slept badly. Rita was worrying about Mohal and how he would cope with the curfew and restrictions placed on him, whether he had set his alarm to make sure he got to the police station for 11am the next day, and what her parents would say when they arrived back. Mohal was reliving the questioning he had undergone. There had been three different police teams as far as he could make out and, although the solicitors did their best to make them go at a steady pace and allow him breaks, he could tell the police were under pressure to get a result and they hounded him about his contacts, his friends, his beliefs, whether anything had changed recently, had he converted? they said. Mohal found he could not get the scenes out his mind when his closed his eyes. Bandhu, meanwhile, lying in Nayan's bed, had found the Star Wars posters not conducive to a peaceful night; the storm troopers were particularly unrestful and he had slept fitfully.

The trio chase cereal round bowls of milk then, while Rita is loading the dishwasher and the men are preparing to leave for the police station and the appointment with Mr Beresford, Jahi's car draws up outside the house and out climb Rita's parents and her younger brother.

"Let me look at you!" Padma says immediately, going to

embrace her older son.

"You've lost weight!" ('Thanks', thinks Rita, 'I did try to feed him up on cheese on toast'.) "And I'm not sure about that beard, I think you need to shave it off before you have to go back to court." His mother adds.

Mohal winces at her attention but is clearly pleased to see her.

Jahi stands close. "Son, we will do something about this." Then, to Bandhu and Mohal, "How are you getting to the police station? Can I come too?" even though he is clearly tired after the flight. They shrug their agreement. The more support the better at the moment they both think.

"Yo, dude!" says Nayan, "Totally awesome! Let me see." He begs to look at the tag on Mohal's leg. Then high fives his brother in congratulation. Mohal says "It's not really cool you know. You never want to be in the dock in court, it's horrible."

"Can't wait to tell my mates." Nayan rejoins.

"Now Nayan." this from Jahi. "We talked about this on the way home. Don't go saying things to your friends. It may make things worse for your brother. We need to keep a low profile."

Then the men are gone. Mohal, sitting in the back of Bandhu's Prius notices that their exit is observed by the occupants of a dark VW Golf parked across the road from 10 Elm Drive. Rita is left with her mother and brother, the former tutting about the state of the kitchen ('You should have seen it yesterday' thinks Rita), the latter bemoaning the absence of the Xbox. ("Where's it gone?".) Neither seems to have realised that since Mohal's arrest normal life has been on hold; the usual rules have ceased to apply.

Bandhu drops off Mohal and Jahi and drives to his own home, his babysitting of Mohal and Rita no longer being needed now his brother and sister in law have returned from India. He promises to keep in touch and to be available to help at any time.

The visit to the police station has brought home to Jahi the reality of the situation.

"They were barely civil!" he says when they return home to Elm Drive by taxi, "They treated Mohal like he's been found guilty already!" His father is so full of righteous indignation that Mohal decides not to mention the car outside the occupants of which seemed to take an interest in their return. It was a red Renault Meganne this time, but Mohal had spent enough time in a police station in the last week to realise that the observers were police officers.

"I expect they were only doing their job." says Rita trying to mollify her father. "What did Mr Beresford have to say?"

"He is going to think which barrister would be best for the case. The police are waiting for more information from the post mortem, the exact time of death is not clear apparently, and they need to get the forensic reports on the scene, and on the equipment and paint they took from the house."

"I can't believe they took the paint!" Jahi adds after a pause, clutching his head with his hand, as if that was the final indignity.

"As it's the weekend they are not expecting more news until Monday at the earliest." Jahi tries to recall everything; having recently returned to the country he feels he is catching up all the time.

"They seem to have concluded Mohal does not present a terrorist or security issue, thank goodness, although they are still digging around. They are treating it as the work of an individual and concentrating on some personal motive. That Mohal was upset about Mr Halliwell's opposition to Syrian charities, or failure to support people who go there for humanitarian reasons. It's very weak but the trouble is, if a prosecution decides to look at your character they will find some mud to throw and Mr Beresford says that Mohal's contacts at University could be cast as suspicious, as could some of the views he has expressed about the police and about government policy on Syria. The best defence would be to show that Mohal couldn't have carried out the murder and couldn't have done the vandalism. The problem is he has no alibi for any of those time frames." Jahi summarises for the family as he sits at the kitchen table.

'Assuming we know the time frame,' thinks Rita, 'Doubt about the time of death does not help.'

* * *

Saturday, 26th October 2013 (evening)

When their parents and younger brother have gone to bed, tired after their journey and with trying to catch up with what has been happening to Mohal. Rita and her older brother sit in the living room, idly watching a comedy film but not really paying it any attention. Rita never thought she would be so glad to have Mohal's company.

"Not sleeping well?" Rita asks. She has seen the dark circles under Mohal's eyes.

He shrugs acknowledgement.

"Where were you that morning, that lunchtime? Before you found Mr Halliwell? You have to tell me Mohal." Rita presses her brother.

Anguished, he replies, his hands squeezed between his knees.

"I can't Rita." then, quieter, "I can't."

"I want to help you, Mohal," Rita pleads, leaning closer to her brother. "We all do. I can't help you if you don't tell me. Tell me and then we'll decide what to do." she tries.

Mohal looks around the room as if wishing he could escape, be anywhere but there.

"I don't know. I can't say… It will cause a lot of trouble." is what he manages to say.

('More trouble than you're in now?', thinks Rita, 'accused of murder?' She wants to say this but holds back, it won't encourage her brother to speak. Give him space, she has learnt that much over the years.)

"She'll get into terrible trouble if I say... her family... her parents ..." Mohal suddenly stutters.

(She? Rita sits up. So there's a girl involved?)

"Not if she's helping you, surely?" Rita tries, "What can be worse than a murder charge?" she adds.

Mohal looks at his sister under his eyes. He stares steadily at her.

"You have no idea." he says slowly.

"Well tell me then!" Rita begs him. "Tell me so I understand."

"I can't. I can't "he repeats in anguish." If anyone finds out..."

"Well, maybe they don't have to." Rita offers. "But you must tell me who she is, how I can find her, how I can clear your name."

"Please. You have to make sure her family never know..."

"Okay, I'll do my best," Rita tries to reassure. "I'll talk to Mr Beresford about what's possible. Now, who is she?"

"Well..." Mohal is reluctant to say, "Her name is... it's Husna Mohammed."

"She's a Muslim girl?" Rita cannot help herself, her surprise is profound. Why would Mohal be seeing a Muslim girl? Not only would their own parents no doubt be furious, Rita knows from Muslim girls at school that their families usually strongly oppose liaisons with any man, let alone non-Muslims. In her experience, most would regard this as a failure and a dishonour to the family. Even liberal Muslim families would be unlikely to countenance a connection with someone who was Hindu; polytheistic traditions were seen as anathema and a marriage with a Hindu would be unthinkable, Rita knows.

"Gosh!" she says, then realising this is not encouraging Mohal to tell his story, she changes her tone.

"So how did you meet her? Where does she live? Where do you two hang out?"

Now she has asked too many questions and Mohal, who is regretting giving Rita the girl's name, looks confused as to which question to answer first. He opts for telling his story in his own words.

"She lives near Aunty Gee in Neasden. We met on the bus. She dropped her Oyster card and didn't notice. I picked it up. Turns out she works at Guy's and Thomas's hospital which is in Westminster, near where I work - worked. That's why she was on the bus. She's a records clerk."

Mohal pauses for breath. Now he has decided to talk he finds he can barely stop. "I won't tell you where she lives or how to get hold of her unless you tell me her family won't find out."

"So how long have you known her?" Rita asks, thinking 'it can't be long, Mohal has only been working in London for about two months'.

"A few weeks." her brother says. "We talk on the bus and we meet at lunchtimes when we can. Sometimes I meet her at the hospital, sometimes we walk in St James' Park. That's all it is. We know we have to be careful. Her family would go mad if they knew she was seeing me."

"What do you mean by 'seeing her'?" Rita asks sharply. "Have you kissed? Anything more?"

"How can you ask me that?" Mohal is offended. "I couldn't put her in danger. We haven't done anything that… that a brother and sister wouldn't do, well maybe we held hands a couple of times. Oh how can I talk about this to you?" Exasperated, he stands and starts pacing the room.

"You're not to tell Mum and Dad, understand?!" he shouts down at Rita who remains sitting, thinking 'he'll wear himself out in a minute'.

"Okay." she says. "Right now I'm the only hope you've got. Tell me about her and I'll talk to Mr Beresford, see what might be possible. I'll speak to him on a hypothetical basis…" she offers.

"Okay." Mohal breathes out deeply and stares at the garden. "Let's go in the kitchen and open the garden doors since I can't go out there. Then I'll tell you."

Brother and sister open the doors from the kitchen to the garden and settle on chairs just inside the house, a sort of small defiance, as close to the edge as they dare.

"She's lovely, Rita, you'd really like her. Funny and clever and so…so…organised…so practical" ('So not like her brother at all then' Rita thinks.)

"She must be good at her job, she has all the right skills. She says a lot of people who are record clerks really want to do something else - work abroad, be a DJ, write a book - but she enjoys it, making sure the notes are kept in order and turn up at the right Department at the right time. When something goes wrong they often ask her to sort it out." He adds proudly.

"You say you've been to the hospital?" Rita queries.

"Yes, I pop in now and then, It's just over the bridge opposite the old County Hall, near where the aquarium is?" he checks Rita recalls this, it was a favourite place to visit when she was younger.

"And you have lunch and walk in the park?" Rita clarifies.

"Yes." her brother says. "She's 20; the same age as me, and can't go to uni, her parents won't hear of it, they think she doesn't need more education."

"Oh no." says Rita, "Not that old chestnut. That's what Al-Qaeda say. Look how they tried to stop Mullala having an education!"

"Well it's not just that. And not all Muslims take that view. A lot of the teachings are about equality, actually." Mohal tries to explain.

"Yeah, well, tell that to the Taliban! Anyway, I'm interrupting you." she says.

"Her family think if Husna went to University she'd meet the wrong people." ('People like you, you mean,' thinks Rita.)

"The plan is – their plan is - for her to marry a cousin in Pakistan. She hasn't met him yet." he explains

"How does she feel about that?" Rita cannot help asking, although they are straying from the immediate problem of Mohal's future liberty. (Her own parents have never said who they would like her to marry, although Rita suspects they would prefer to find a husband they approve of, but she doubts they would put pressure on her and she would respect anybody they suggested and at least see if she liked them; that's as far as she has got in her thinking because, basically, she is focussed on going to university and getting a job, not a husband!).

"She says she trusts her parents to choose someone suitable and she wants to please them, so she'll meet him if they want and see how she finds him." Mohal explains.

"Oh Rita," he adds, "She's very pretty. Amazing eyes. I do like her a lot."

Rita can see her brother is taken with this girl. 'Let's hope she feels sufficiently strongly about him to help with providing his alibi' she thinks.' What if this Husna is too scared to do so?'

"So on the day in question." Rita brings the conversation round, sounding like a barrister in court questioning a witness.

"On the Tuesday, we met at Victoria Station at 12. We got sandwiches in Boots and walked to St James's Park. We ate our lunch on a bench looking at the ducks and swans. There's a pelican down there too, did you know?"

"So you met at twelve? What time did you leave the office and how long were you together?" Rita is not be deflected by talk of exotic birds.

"I left about 11.30, maybe a little after. She walked back with me from the train station and I left her at the staff entrance of PCH at 1.45. She was on a late shift, not due at the hospital until 2.00. I got back in time for the meeting on Mr Halliwell's schedule. The one the police say was for 12.15 whereas I know it was for 2.15, that's what Camilla told me." Mohal tries to tell Rita what happened.

"Did anyone see you when you were together?" Rita probes.

"No, that's the whole point. We don't want to be seen by anyone who knows us. Husna's family live and work in Neasden so they are never in that part of London, thank goodness, but even so there are risks. Her brother runs a mini-cab firm so never - promise me this, never - mention this when you are in a mini-cab and never take a mini-cab with Husna if you do meet her. You never know if the information is going to be passed on, it's like a secret network."

'Oh dear.' thinks Rita, 'More conspiracy theories. Mohal is fond of those!'

"I'll speak to Mr Beresford and see if there's a way of getting her evidence without disclosing who she is." she tries. "And if you tell me how, I'll try to see if Husna will meet me, somewhere safe."

"Don't reveal her name." cautions Mohal "Just in case. I'm so afraid. I don't know her family but you read such dreadful things. She says a cousin disappeared in mysterious circumstances. Just never came back to school after the summer holidays, when she was 15. The rumours were that she'd gone to Pakistan and killed herself when her parents insisted she marry a man she'd never met. But Husna doesn't know if that's actually true." Mohal is trembling now and Rita thinks maybe they should shut the doors. It may be the cold air or it may be fear for Husna that is causing her brother to shake.

"If you do see Husna," Mohal's voice is weak, "Tell her, tell her I am thinking of her?"

Giving Rita Husna's mobile number, and strict instructions on how to contact her – "only use text, only text between 10pm and 6am, tell her you are 'Mo's sister' so she knows you know me. I expect she is worried, if she's seen the arrest on the news"- Mohal feels anxious in the pit of his stomach. Has he got Husna into trouble? He does not want his freedom at the expense of causing her problems with her family. Before he settles down to sleep that night he recalls a text from the Qur'an the imam told him.

Do they not know that it is God who accepts the repentance of his servants?

Chapter

9

"You have sat too long for any good you have been doing lately… depart, I say, and let us have done with you.In the name of God, go!"

Oliver Cromwell's address
to the Rump Parliament
20th April 1653.

Sunday, 27th October 2013

Almost everyone gets up early for breakfast; even though it is Sunday and the dental clinic is closed, even though Mohal only needs to leave the house to get to the police station for 11am, even though Rita has no school that day or the next; it is as if they all feel tense and as if they should be doing something about the situation. Only Nayan sleeps on as the other four sit round the table at 8am in the white modern kitchen, looking out at a day which is so young it has not yet decided what weather to deliver.

Padma offers muesli and toast and herself settles down to a yoghurt and a banana. She has no particular plans for the day, which is unlike her. She had spent the fortnight before their trip to India buying ingredients and baking them so that Rita would have tasty healthy dishes to eat while they were away. Now they are back unexpectedly early she has lost her bearings. Should they start on the prepared meals? Or would the meals be needed at another time, in which case should she cook some more? Padma, who is sure that extra lines have appeared on her forehead since the news of Mohal's arrest, realises she is not eating, just pushing the pieces of fruit backwards and forwards in the bowl with her spoon while she tries to orient herself and her day. It seems like there is an enormous chasm of fear and uncertainty in front of her and she cannot see how to get across.

No one speaks. Like characters in a silent movie they stand up and sit down, walk to the fridge or the kettle, glance outside hoping the weather will do something, that there may be something interesting to see or talk about, something to distract them. Mohal is feeling guilty at the worry he is causing, and worrying that his freedom may never be returned. Jahi, whose hair has started to show grey at the edges, like his father's did, he recalls, is feeling powerless and is unsure what his role is in this drama, how can he best help his son?

Rita lays down the toast she has been trying to eat. Her mouth is too dry for her to chew it. Her conversation with Mohal last night has been playing through her head like a tune you cannot get rid of. She has exchanged texts with Husna, she hopes safely, and clears her throat to make her announcement. Looking across the table at Mohal she says, "Mum, Dad, I may be going to London later, to help Mr Beresford. I'll give him a call in an hour or so and then make arrangements."

Jahi puts down his cup, Padma drops her spoon in her bowl.

"Help him?" Jahi says, "How?"

"I can't exactly say." Rita says slowly.

"What about school?" Padma objects.

"I'm going to try to help him collect some evidence." Rita explains, "It's an inset day tomorrow so I don't need to be in school. I'll stay with Aunty Gee in Neasden again, if she'll have me."

"What are you getting yourself into? Should I come with you?" says Jahi, wanting to take action but then glancing at Mohal whom he is due to take to the police station later that morning. Now he feels torn between his children, whom should he support?

Rita was afraid of this. "No, no." she says adamantly, "I'll be fine on my own and Mr Beresford won't want two of us under his feet. I'll call you all the time so you know where I am." She hopes this is enough to calm her parents' fears, she knows that Husna will only meet if Rita is alone. Before anyone can say any more she leaves the table to pack an overnight bag and prepare to make her phone call. Padma moves her bowl to the dishwasher, looking less than convinced. Mohal follows his sister out of the room.

In the hallway, Rita has a whispered conversation with her older brother which is not lost on her parents but they deem it wise not to interfere. Whatever Rita is doing she has her brother's interests at heart and it is beyond them to know how to help him, they think. "Whatever it is Rita." Jahi says as he passes them on his way to the staircase "Make sure you are safe. I don't want two children on the wrong side of the police."

"I'll be okay." says Rita, "Call Mr Beresford if you like."

"I may do that." her father retorts over his shoulder, thinking he will call her bluff.

At 10.15am Jahi and Mohal leave the house for the police station in the City centre. Padma has made clear she wants Mohal to allow at least 30 minutes extra before his deadlines, so she wants him to be at the police station for 10.30am every day and back at the house by 8.30pm at the latest. She is very afraid of the consequences if he breaches his bail conditions by a second, and does not want to draw attention to their situation. So far there have been no reporters, she is glad to note, although she has seen strange cars parked near the house, which is unusual. The neighbours do not seem to have realised there is anything untoward going on she is relieved to find. But how long can they keep up appearances? No wonder all the family are on edge and anxious.

"Well what do they do in Parliament all day?" Nayan had

asked his brother the previous evening when the curfew had begun and they were in the living room deciding to record *Match of the Day* so they could watch it together the next day, Nayan feeling his eyes drooping with tiredness… "All I ever see is that Speaker dude trying to make them be quiet and shouting 'order order'" he mimics Speaker Bercow's voice.

Rita had chimed in with her historical information, as usual, telling them all that the Speaker's role started in 1377 with Thomas Hungerford, although there had been someone presiding over discussions of councils before that, including a Peter de Montfort who presided over the gathering in Oxford on 1258 which was sometimes, she told them to Nayan's amusement, known as the "Mad Parliament". The Speaker even has an official residence, she informed her family, which is at the Westminster Bridge end of the Palace of Westminster (not far from the scene of Mohal's arrest, but she did not add this detail.)

Mohal had nodded agreement to this and explained to his brother that MPs debate motions in the House of Commons and that Peers do so in the House of Lords. He quoted a former Speaker, Baroness Boothroyd.

"The function of Parliament is to hold the executive to account… It is in Parliament in the first instance that Ministers must explain and justify their policies."

The Lords do more careful scrutiny of legislative proposals, he told his brother and the Commons is more noticeably party political in its approach. Sometimes the debate subjects are put forward by the Government and sometimes they are proposed by the Opposition or individual MPs. Nayan was particularly taken with the information that there are lines in the carpet in the House of Commons to ensure Government and Opposition members keep at least two swords' length apart. The purpose is to talk, or 'parley', as Rita told them, not to fight to resolve differences. "The Chamber is rarely as busy as you see it for Prime Minister's questions," Mohal had said, "as MPs have lots of other things to do – sitting on Committees, meeting constituents and interest groups, replying to correspondence" he added proudly, "That's where I help… helped."

Mohal went on "Sometimes they are making or changing the law and sometimes they are checking what the Government are doing, so there are special debates to question the different Ministers… And there is a lot of voting" Mohal explained, "They have to physically walk through the correct lobby – there's no electronic voting like in other Parliaments."

"No!" Nayan was astonished, he could not imagine a process that does not involve computers, they are an integral part of his everyday life.

Now Mohal, sitting in his father's car, having noticed the car near the house today is the red Renault again, has his fingers metaphorically crossed for the success of Rita's mission and is recalling what she had said just before they left. She had been busy on her phone since the lacklustre breakfast at the start of the day. She told her brother that she had called Mr Beresford at his home. "Haylo!" was the way he answered the phone, apparently, making 'hello' into a funny sound. He had been pleased for Mohal's sake that there was the chance of alibi evidence and said that, if the witness – "Don't worry I didn't give her name, I didn't even say it was a woman." Rita assured her brother - is willing, they can provide a redacted statement.

"A what?" asked Mohal.

"You know, with all the bits that might identify the person crossed out." Rita explained.

"Oh". Mohal said doubtfully.

"The police, the CPS and the judge would need to know who she was but keep it confidential." Rita affirmed.

"You're sure?" Mohal checked.

"Yes, that's how it works. If she had to give evidence in

person" she hesitated as she saw the look of horror on her brother's face "If she had to" she emphasised "It would be behind a screen. To protect her anonymity. But with luck, if we show you couldn't have been there, the CPS will have to drop the case and police will have to find the real killer." Rita tried to remember all that Mr Beresford had said.

"I hope you are right." Mohal had sighed and shaken his head.

"The first thing is for me to meet Husna and persuade her to give evidence." Rita said.

That was the second call. Rita had left a message on Husna's phone late last night, and the girl had rung back that morning. The two are to meet on Monday.

Chapter

10

"When they are 50 yards from Parliament Hill they are no longer honourable members, they are just nobodies."
Pierre Trudeau, Canadian Prime Minister

Monday, 28th October 2013 11.30 am

Rita follows Mohal's directions on leaving the tube station at Victoria, although this is difficult to do. Most of the immediate area seems to be under demolition and reconstruction. A group of cranes – red, green, silver, like giant crayons pointing to the sky - stands on a large square area of grey and brown rubble. At eye level there are temporary barriers and wire mesh- sided walkways which govern where pedestrians can cross the road. Eventually she establishes she is on Victoria Street and then she can see the House of Fraser store, just past Boots, and she realises she is at the other end of the street where she had met Mr Beresford on Thursday. As she walks along she is aware of a clearing in an area to her right between the shops and offices; looking up from the pavement and the rows of people moving towards her, she sees the striped terracotta and white bricked beauty of Westminster Cathedral, like a piece of Italy transplanted to central London to sit between drab grey shop and office buildings. Tourists and worshippers are passing in and out and people are sitting in the square in front of the building. But she has no time for tourist attractions and presses on her way, resuming her confrontation with pedestrians determinedly striding towards her.

As she walks, Rita is both buoyed and daunted by her telephone conversation with Mr Beresford earlier that day.

The lawyer told her that a senior pathologist had reviewed the evidence at the request of the MP's family and the thinking was now that Mr Halliwell had been stabbed around 12 o'clock, not later as had been thought. Apparently his heart had stopped almost immediately. So his heart had stopped beating nearly 2 hours before Mohal found him! That had to be helpful Rita thinks.

Mr Beresford had wished her luck with the witness. Rita had told him about the walk Mohal says he made and suggested that CCTV evidence or mobile phone records might support his story but Mr Beresford had been pessimistic. He said it was unlikely the Legal Services Commission would pay the costs of searching through CCTV to find Mohal where he says he was. "It's all about cost now." he said "We have to find a cheap way to get the evidence we need to clear him." Nevertheless, Rita cannot help looking round for CCTV cameras as she walks along; 'maybe there will be a way', she thinks.

Rita goes into the first entrance to the store she reaches and looks around. The Caffè Nero, where she has arranged to meet Husna, is on the basement level her brother has told her, where menswear is displayed. Rita realises the escalator going downwards is behind a range of women's clothes. Trying hard to ignore the apricot coloured lace top in front of her (she thinks it would look great with her leggings) she steps onto the moving stairs and at the bottom finds herself in a display of mens jeans and shirts; she can make out the café entrance beyond a display of sweaters.

The seating area is dimly lit and various tables and benches are occupied, mostly with people who look like they are snatching a few minutes from work, or not even escaping as several are talking on phones or dealing with emails as they munch. Rita spots Husna in the far left corner, sipping a glass of fruit juice through a straw. Rita waves tentatively and gets a shy wave of the fingers in return.

"Hi, I'm Rita." she says as she makes for the table.

"Husna." the other girl replies.

"I'll just get a tea and join you." Rita says. The girl acknowledges with a bat of her long lashes. ('She is pretty, Mohal was right!' Rita thinks). She has clear, healthy looking skin (no sign of spots Rita thinks) and her face is long and lean with high cheek bones. Her eyes are large almond shapes accentuated by skillful makeup but Rita can see no cosmetics are needed to make Husna attractive; she is naturally very beautiful. On her head she wears a blue and green floral scarf over a black headdress so that no hair can be seen at all. The scarf cascades over her shoulders where it meets a black long sleeved tunic worn over a maxi length black skirt. The effect is elegant and understated, but somehow covering herself with this simplicity emphasises the girl's innate beauty.

Rita returns with a mug of tea and some wafer biscuits.

"Thanks for agreeing to see me." she says as she takes off her jacket and sits down opposite Husna. The basement of the shop has no natural light and is very warm. Rita wonders how the assistants cope with it all day long.

"Mohal is in trouble?" Husna sounds genuinely concerned. Rita explains how Mr Halliwell has been killed and how Mohal, as the person who found the body, has been accused.

"But the police are now certain the murder occurred around 12 o'clock. Mr Halliwell's heart had stopped for about two hours before Mohal found him." Rita presses on, then hesitates as she sees Husna shudder. After a pause she takes a breath and then resumes, "So if you can vouch for where Mohal was between 12.00 and 1.45 they'll have to let him go!" she rushes to the end of what she wants to say, then sits back to sip her tea, watching the other girl's face ripple in the steam of her tea which rises over the rim of her mug.

"How is he?" Husna wants to know.

Rita says he's bearing up and explains the bail conditions.

"That's why he can't email you." she explains.

"Oh we never email" Husna says quickly. "That's too easily intercepted. We have to be so careful." she adds. "My family are very strict and believe the words *'Whenever a man is alone with a woman, Satan is the third among them'*. They would not want me to know a Hindu as the Qu'ran says *'They are not lawful wives for unbelievers, nor are the unbelievers lawful husbands for them.'*"

Rita shudders. 'Has she come all this way only for Husna to quote her religion and turn her down?' she thinks.

Suddenly the other girl speaks again.

"So if I give a statement to the police they can guarantee my family won't know? Won't find out about Mohal?" she asks, talking carefully and slowly, in contrast to Rita's enthusiastic energetic tones. "Here." she says, "I say this every day for him." And she hands Rita a prayer written on a white index card; in careful, looping script.It says -

Prayer for Protection

"Prophet Muhammad (peace be upon him)

O God, you are my Lord. There is none worthy of worship except You. I rely on You and You are the Great Lord of the Throne. Whatever God wills happens, and whatever He does not will does not happen.There is no power or strength except by God. I know that God is able to do anything, and that God knows all. O God I seek refuge in You from the evil in myself and every creature that You have given power over us. Verily my Lord is on the straight path."

* * *

Monday, 28th October 2013 12.30pm

When Husna has gone, Rita rises slowly from the table they had shared, tucking the prayer card into her Cath Kidston bag, her thoughts and ideas cascading like a large waterfall in a rush of exciting but potentially dangerous energy. She could almost hear the roar of the ideas in her ears. What to do with what Husna has told her? How to rescue Mohal and protect Husna at the same time? Who should she call? How should she tell the story? It was all hopeful and hopeless at the same time.

Heedless of her surroundings, Rita retraces her journey through menswear, almost stumbling by mistake onto the down escalator coming towards her before realising her error and passing across the sales floor to the staircase which is moving up to the floor above. Emerging once more into the hot, glasshouse, perfumed, atmosphere of the ground floor she barely notices the over made-up assistants lying in wait to assail her with their perfumes and she exits to Victoria Street via the nail bar where several clients relax and recline like patients, their hands extended for beauty-saving treatment.

Turning right on the busy street, Rita wanders absentmindedly to the pelican crossing where her unconscious mind halts her at the kerb and then allows her to be swept across with the crowd when the lights change. Rita dodges to right and left like a netball player, to avoid the people coming towards her, mostly tourists with cameras swinging round their necks or iPads held aloft in order that no view of London should be left unfilmed.

Rita presses on, trying to find a way out of the labyrinth of her thoughts. It is only as she reaches the corner with Great Smith Street that she realises where her legs are taking her. Ahead, eloquent in its stature and calm presence amid the bustle, stands the pale giant that is the twin towered Westminster Abbey, more imposing and impressive than any of the modern buildings being thrown up along Victoria Street, and which were no doubt destined to be demolished just as quickly while the Abbey would continue its timeless occupation. Rita queues to pay and enters the cool, tall, memorial-filled walls of the Abbey, feeling immediately that here is a place where she can unscramble her mind.

As she stalks around, in search of familiar names on the plaques, she reaches Poets' corner where she finds a plaque to Jane Austen (who, she knows, is buried in Winchester Cathedral), a bust to William Blake made by Sir Jacob Epstein and a tablet to Charlotte, Emily and Anne Bronte on the wall next to Shakespeare's memorial. ('The place is like a Waterstones for the dead!' she thinks, 'so many famous writers are commemorated here'.) There is a memorial stone to Lord Byron which sits near memorials to Dylan Thomas, Lewis Carol and DH Lawrence. Geoffrey Chaucer is one of those writers actually buried in the Abbey, she finds, as are Samuel Johnson and Alfred Lord Tennyson. There is a bust in memory of Coleridge on a pillar above Wordsworth's statue. Charles Dickens, as Rita reads he apparently requested, has his grave marked by a small stone inscribed in plain English letters. Keats and Shelly, Rita finds, have identical oval tablets to commemorate them.

In another part of the Abbey, Rita comes across a small modern stone which records that Oliver Cromwell was briefly buried at the Abbey before being disinterred and buried under Tyburn Gallows (near Marble Arch) when Charles II was restored to the throne. Former Prime Ministers whose memorials Rita spots include Neville Chamberlain, Sir Winston Churchill, David Lloyd George, and Sir Robert Peel. Spencer Perceval, the only Prime Minister to be assassinated in the House of Commons, has a memorial on a window ledge in the nave; Rita pauses before this and wonders if there will ever be a memorial to Mervyn Halliwell, somehow she thinks not. Spencer Perceval she recalls was shot and killed by an unbalanced man who had a grievance against the government; was that the motive for killing Mr Halliwell? Would the police even find such a person if they continue to be convinced that Mohal is guilty?

Rita also hunts out Royal burials - Edward the Confessor, of course, who first built the Abbey and the imposing marble tomb of Henry III who revered Edward and rebuilt large parts of the Abbey to produce the French Gothic masterpiece it remains today. A gilt bronze effigy of Henry III lies serenely, his head on a bronze pillow. Elizabeth I in her white marble monument in the Lady Chapel was the last monarch to be buried in the Abbey with a monument erected above her. Her burial, and the reburial of Mary Queen of Scots in another magnificent marble tomb in the Lady Chapel, were arranged by King James I Rita reads.

In St Edmund's Chapel, Rita is impressed with the memorial to Frances Brandon, Duchess of Suffolk, mother of Lady Jane Grey, 'the nine day queen' who lived at Bradgate Park in Leicestershire. She is shown resplendent, lying on a rush mattress with a lion at her feet and wearing an ermine-lined mantle over her dress with a pendant round her neck. Finally Rita finds what she is looking for, the carved and painted shield of Simon de Montfort, Earl of Leicester, which is in the north choir aisle. She must tell Priya! This shows that de Montfort and Henry were not always enemies, they worked together too, and Simon was a trusted adviser until he started to oppose the King. The shield is one of a series which shows the donors towards the building of Henry III's new Abbey. Rita knows de Montfort is not buried in the Abbey since he was killed in battle at Evesham and buried in the Abbey there.

As she wanders the long aisles recalling the TV pictures of Prince William's wedding in the Abbey, Rita thinks that although Henry III might have been regarded as a weak King he had created a lasting monument through his piousness and identification with Edward the Confessor. He had achieved more than many other monarchs who preferred fighting.

Leaving the Abbey, Rita's mind has started to clear. She

turns towards some more familiar landmarks, taking out her phone and calling Inspector Jamie Bridge as she walks along. First she passes the Houses of Parliament with Big Ben standing next to it, managing to look a little unreal because it is so familiar, it is hard to believe it is not a model. Rita sees queues outside the St Stephen's entrance as the public try to glimpse the House of Commons in action. Mohal has described the feeling of walking through the magnificent building made famous by its frequent television appearances. The lobby where the two Houses meet is where the TV reporters often stand importantly while people of all types, MPs and Lords, constituents and advisers, pass hurriedly across or meet to discuss issues or tactics.

Walking to Westminster tube station Rita catches sight of Portcullis House on Victoria Embankment. This is a modern take on the gothic style. She walks up to inspect the main entrance, where she sees the conveyor belt for the airline style security system and uniformed officers checking visitors' bags. There is a seating area near the window where visitors can wait and further back, astonishingly, Rita can see rows of trees amid lines of marble troughs . These make the building look more like a greenhouse than a place of business she thinks. Rita walks round to the staff entrance at the side and then retraces her steps and crosses Victoria Embankment, glancing down to the ground on the traffic island at the spot where her brother was detained. She finds the bridge over the river has a low green parapet. It is possible to lean over it. Easy to see how Mohal might have tried to be sick there. Also how the police might think he had thrown a weapon into the fast moving Thames. It was unlikely that any search would find a knife disposed of in that way, unless at some point it happened to wash up lower down the river's course, she ponders; so much of protecting Mohal is about proving what did not occur! 'At least I know where it all happened.' she thinks as she crosses back over the spot where her brother was publicly arrested and measures with her eyes the distance to the bridge and the river.

* * *

Monday, 28th October 2013 5pm

Catching the tube from Westminster to Embankment and then travelling on the Northern line to Euston, Rita emerges onto a confusing concourse with buses spinning in and out, conflicting lines of pedestrians moving across each other like a complicated country dance, the luggage and children and dogs scattered around presenting a continuing challenge to avoid tripping up. The open expanse, teeming with people and activity, leads to the noise and rush of the Euston Road. The traffic moves and queues in fits and starts, racing and crawling alternately as the sets of traffic lights change. Ambulance sirens pierce the hum of traffic at frequent intervals and suddenly the cacophony is added to by fire engines emerging from the fire station,red and glorious in their quest, like knights going into battle.

Reaching the British Library, Rita finds sanctuary. The red brick building rises like a cruise ship moored in the garden area where people of all kinds - old, young, smart, casual, many with laptop bags on their shoulders or books in their hands - stand, or sit on the low walls and benches, in the soothing open area conducive to preparing visitors for the quiet orderliness of the library itself. People chat in groups of two or three or sip coffee silently, contemplating the scene or avidly consuming their reading material.

Rita steps through the glazed entrance, smiling at the security guard who smiles back and waves her through. She spots ahead on her left the Treasures of the British Library in the Sir John Ritblat Gallery and heads up the stairs straight there. Resisting the temptation to dally by Jane

Austen's writing desk, various Shakespeare folios, exotically illuminated manuscripts,handwritten pages by Dickens and many other exhibits which excite her, Rita makes for the area set aside for Magna Carta where she is relieved to see only a few people are gathered, mostly Americans and Japanese she notes.

With a shiver of expectation she steps into the exhibition area and there, under glass, are the other two copies of Magna Carta. She has now seen all four! It is all she can do not to clap her hands to applaud herself, so she metaphorically pats herself on the back instead. Once again the Latin writing is small as if an insect has trailed across the page, but in very straight, even, lines. The exhibition explains some of the history of the charter and its later significance and application. The USA especially revere it as the founding idea for their Bill of Rights; the settlers were keen that freedoms won in England should not be lost in the New World. Rita sighs as she looks as these twin offspring of a struggle between the barons and the king 800 years ago. Happy she has achieved her objective, Rita leaves the quiet atmosphere of the British Library and crosses Midland Road to enter the glass construction which is St Pancras station to wait for her train back to Leicester.

* * *

Monday, 28th October 2013 9.30pm

Padma and Nayan have gone up to bed, Mohal is in his room, trying to read and anxious to hear from Rita. Jahi sits at the end of the kitchen nearest the garden, alone in the darkness - lit only by one uplighter so he looks like he is appearing in a one man play. He is staring at his garden but the night has covered it and he is not really looking anyway. He is thinking – worrying - about his eldest child. He could wring the necks of the police who have got this so badly wrong, who think his son could be capable of... he would rather not think about it, and he knows that violence is not the answer, he abhors it and so does Mohal, that is why this makes no sense.

Jahi has spoken with various friends since the arrest and got the benefit of their advice, such as it is. Most wanted to change the subject as soon as possible, as if being arrested and charged is something contagious. A couple have offered the names of lawyers but Jahi is content that Mr Beresford and his contacts are doing their best. One friend suggested a media campaign – get on Twitter! Free Mohal! – but Jahi is afraid that may do more harm than good, dragging his son's name into the public arena and exposing him to those internet trolls you hear so much about these days. If only there was something he could do. He feels powerless. While Mohal is under house detention and he goes to work and drills peoples' teeth the wheels of justice are turning and who knew what would happen next?

In the car to the police station that day, suppressing a feeling that they were being followed, he was sure he had seen that red car before, he had asked Mohal to explain some of his views. It turned out that Mohal was very indignant about the death of Abbas Kahn in Syria and the British Government's failure to get him freed. Dr Kahn, he told his father, was starved and tortured by the Syrian authorities, accused of terrorism when he was helping civilians – women and children. "And our Government didn't do anything to help him!" Mohal was outraged. He thought the Assad regime had killed Kahn to stop him telling the world about their atrocities and that the UK Government could have prevented it.

"At least you will get a fair trial." he had tried to placate his son, only to be greeted by "Don't tell me they don't fabricate evidence! I bet they are doing that now!"

"How can you say that?" Jahi was outraged, surely that

would not happen here?

"Look at that guy Nitin Shah." his older son had retorted," He was a trainee solicitor charged with verbally abusing a female bar manager. Turns out a City of London police officer forged the signature of the alleged victim. Then the IPCC – the independent police complaints commission - allowed the City of London to investigate itself! Shah had to bring proceedings and wrote to the IPCC" (Mohal has recalled his exact words Jahi was both impressed and alarmed to note)

"As an Asian I have had to endure disgustingly poor service from this corrupt police force which demonstrates that nothing had changed since the Stephen Lawrence case."

Mohal paused "So can you blame me for thinking they are trying to fit me up?" his son had finished belligerently.

Jahi did not enter into further discussion but prayed they would be able to afford a good barrister and that they could find the evidence that would prove Mohal innocent.

Now Jahi, waiting for his daughter, thinks Rita has some ideas which she won't discuss with him. Jahi smiles wryly to himself. How did he end up with two such different children? Mohal is indignant at injustice but lazy and dreamlike, effortless in his ability to while away the time, and Rita is less resentful but busy and full of practical ideas, restless to be active. What about Nayan? What effect will this have on him? No doubt at school tomorrow he will boast about his brother's tag and probably exaggerate the facts, making out that Mohal has been more badly treated than he has. But will his friends support him or shun him? Will the whole family be regarded with suspicion? Jahi begins to wonder if some patients will start cancelling their appointments when the news emerges. Will the business be affected?

All Jahi knows is that he would do anything to protect his son. If they need money for a good barrister they will mortgage or sell the house if needs be, he bravely resolves to himself, choosing not to think about the look on his wife's face if he were to announce this. She has made improving the house her life's work and the kitchen, only completed last year, is its crowning glory. But their son's liberty must come first. Jahi nods to himself. Rita should be back from her mission in London soon. He hopes it has been successful. She was very vague on the telephone and seemed to spend most of her time at tourist sites around Victoria as far as he could make out.

* * *

Tim Beresford is back in Leicester, working late at the offices of Beresford, Maitland and Maclean in New Walk, in the centre of the City (branches in Wigston, Oadby and Great Glen). He has been ringing round the chambers of barristers he knows, and some suggested by the London agents, but without any success so far. As a student, Mohal qualifies for Legal Aid but despite the 'cab rank' rule barrister's clerks were proving adept at avoiding taking the brief on behalf of their chambers. "Legal aid rates?" they say "Oh no, I'm afraid Mr X, Miss Y, Mrs Z is tied up in a long trial at the moment. Good luck with finding somebody!" It was getting exasperating and Mr Beresford is worried. How to find Mohal Patel good representation? He knows a few Asian lawyers in Nottingham and resolves to pick their brains tomorrow. Perhaps one of them will be sympathetic or able to suggest someone.

If the CPS press ahead, Mr Beresford is thinking, this may be a case where Imran Kahn, who acted in the Stephen Lawrence case, or Gareth Peirce, whose client list is full of people facing terror allegations, like the Birmingham Six and the Guildford Four, would be useful in exposing the miscarriage of justice which he is sure would be about to take place. But how to afford them? And do Mohal and his family want that kind of publicity? It could haunt him for the rest of his life, but at least he could have a chance of freedom. Tim Beresford suddenly envisages 'Free Mohal' marches in Leicester and rallies in Victoria Park. Could that really happen? This case is starting to be a heavy responsibility he thinks.

* * *

Inspector Jamie Bridge is on the late shift, and is sitting at a work station at Leicester police station, looking at the disturbing amount of material appearing on Twitter and other social media about Mervyn Halliwell. Rumours are circulating about wild parties, drunken orgies and homosexual liaisons. No names or details as yet and no one has come forward to lodge any complaints as far as he knows. By tomorrow this will be across the press, however obliquely to protect themselves from Leveson reforms and libel laws. How will Scotland Yard react he wonders?

Jamie Bridge eyes his mobile. He is hoping to receive a phone call from Mohal's alibi witness. The Deputy Commissioner overseeing the investigation in the Metropolitan Police had been less than pleased when he had spoken to her earlier to explain that there was potential alibi evidence for the time of the murder, the sensitivity around the witness for reasons of personal safety, and that a member of the Patel family had persuaded the witness to contact Jamie.

"Why you?" had been the reaction.

"I think the Patel family trust me. I met them before, over something else." Jamie had explained.

"Another murder?" Deputy Commissioner Alison Tate said in clipped tones, sounding more sceptical by the minute. "Is there anything else about this family I should know?"

"No, no." Jamie Bridge reassured her. "The family were helpful in resolving our inquiries, helping us to catch the killer."

"When you say 'family'…" Alison Tate tried to probe.

"No, I'm not going to name names." Jamie Bridge did not wish to draw attention to Rita.

"And this witness, how do we know it's genuine? That the family have not just cooked this up?" The Deputy Commissioner sounding doubtful again.

"Let's wait until we get the statement. Then you and the CPS can look into it. It will have to be handled confidentially and kept anonymous. But it sounds genuine to me. You certainly can't ignore it, Ma'am, the defence would shred you in court if you did."

"Okay." the senior officer had reluctantly accepted the position. "Go ahead and let's see."

After a pause she had added, "And come to the Wednesday briefing. Sergeant Kahn can give you details". The Deputy Commissioner hung up abruptly before Jamie Bridge could accept and he was left looking at his silent phone and wondering what his own boss would say; he had told him to cooperate fully "We want to look good, it's a high profile case." had been his exact words, so presumably he would not begrudge the mileage. As Inspector Bridge recalls this exchange his mobile starts to move across the surface of the work station. He looks at the number calling – yes, this looks like the witness he thinks.

* * *

On the train back home, Rita stands by one of the doors so she can chat to Priya without disturbing other passengers - or customers as the train company calls them -and in order not divulge any secrets about Mohal and his 'friend' to the rest of the carriage, which is half full of scattered,tired looking travellers.

"How did it go?" Priya wants to know. Then, "Is she pretty?"

"Oh yes." Rita acknowledges. "In an Angelina Jolie sort of way." Priya is not reassured by this, you couldn't get prettier than that! She thinks, reaching for her comb as her friend continues.

"Nice too. Quiet, but then she doesn't know me. And she's scared. She's taking a risk helping Mohal." Rita tells Priya.

"They were together, though? That lunch time?" Priya checks.

"Oh yes, no doubt about it. Like Mohal said, they met at the station, wandered about, bought a sandwich."

"Where?" Priya interrupts.

"What?" Rita can barely hear and has to dodge out of the way of the catering trolley as it rattles through to the next carriage, pushed by a young man in black trousers, shirt and turban.

"Where did they get the sandwich? Maybe the shop will remember them, or have CCTV?" Priya explains.

"Good thought." says Rita whose brain has been struggling to cope with all the information she has been acquiring, like an overloaded computer.

"They got back to Portcullis House – where it happened - at 1.45. She remembers Big Ben chiming. Then Husna went to start her shift at the hospital, it's just the other side of the bridge."

"And she'll make a statement?" Priya asks.

"Yes. Husna said she'd give Inspector Bridge a statement on the phone tonight and call in to Scotland Yard in her lunch hour if she has to sign anything. That way her family need never know."

"Fingers crossed!" says Priya. "By the way," she tells Rita, "There's a lot of nasty stuff on Twitter."

"What about?" Rita asks, alarmed. Has Mohal's identity leaked out? she fears.

"About Mr Halliwell. Suggestions he was inappropriate." Priya explains.

"Inappropriate? What do you mean?" Rita is unsure.

"You know," says her friend, "Groping and stuff. Going too far. Getting too close. It seems to be men who are saying this, so far as I can make out."

"Groping?" Rita is astonished, "When would he get the chance?" She thinks MPs are very busy people and always in crowds, from what Mohal has said.

"There are suggestions of parties, hotels, too much drinking." Priya elaborates.

"Do you think any of it's true?" Rita asks.

"Who knows? You can say anything about someone once they're dead, can't you? You can't be sued." Priya reminds her.

"I guess." replies Rita "But if several people are writing this stuff you can't help thinking there's something in it." Something else to tell Tim Beresford when she has finished this call, she thinks, as her train slows down to call at Market Harborough on its way to Leicester.

Chapter

11

"At the House of Commons sword-fighting is strictly taboo. Back-stabbing, on the other hand, is quite a different matter."

Giles Brandreth

Tuesday, 29ᵗʰ October 2013 9pm

Rita, Priya, Nayan and Mohal are in the kitchen at Rita's house, watching, against the girls' wishes but to please Mohal, the Dave channel which is wall to wall *QI* ('at least Nayan might learn something', Rita thinks) and Jeremy Clarkson ('Nayan might learn the wrong things', Rita worries). She had reluctantly switched to Dave when all the news programmes were carrying morbid long lens pictures of the Catholic funeral which had been held for Mervyn Halliwell at the Brompton Oratory in London earlier that day. It was a private family occasion and the press had been kept behind barriers, away from the ceremony. There were suggestions that there might be a memorial service later in the year. In view of the lack of footage of the occasion, the news coverage had concentrated on tracing Mr Halliwell's career and playing speeches he had made and comments he had given in his numerous interviews. These were slanted towards his opposition to the Syrian charities and to people going to Syria to help civilians or fight for the rebels, suggesting the media thought this the likeliest motive, even though the police were not categorising the incident as one of terrorism and their press conferences had repeated that the crime was being treated as a personal one.

"So how long can they keep you on a tag?" Priya asks

Mohal as he joins his sister and her friend in the kitchen of 10 Elm Drive.

"There's really no limit." says Rita, "The police and CPS can drag it out; there are cases where people have been kept like this for months, with the trial date being postponed."

"But that's disgraceful!" says Priya. "That can't be right, to keep you on hold like that!" She is outraged. "Surely your Magna Whatsit has something to say about it?" she asks Rita.

"'Fraid not. There wasn't any tagging in the 13th century unfortunately so they didn't say anything about it. People can be kept in Mohal's situation for a long time. But others are in a worse position in a way."

"What do you mean?" Mohal wants to know, 'what could be worse than being wrongly charged with murder?' he thinks.

"At least they have to set a trial date for you. People can be kept on police bail without charge," his sister explains. "Some people are kept on ice for years, not knowing if they are going to be charged and not able to get on with their lives."

"Does that really happen?" asks Priya.

"Well it happened to Neil Wallis for example, in connection with the phone hacking allegations. He was in limbo for 19 months and never charged, and last year the Law Society gave the example of a man who was on police bail for 3 years 8 months, he did not know whether action against him would be taken for all that time."

"But does it matter?" Priya explores.

"Well, you'd have trouble getting a job with that hanging over you, wouldn't you?" Rita tells her, "And the bail conditions are often accompanied by restrictions."

"Like what?" Mohal asks.

"Well, if there's a financial aspect you might have your assets and bank accounts frozen or property seized. Suggestions of sexual misconduct might get you sacked, for example if you're a teacher, even if you have not been charged."

"So it can really screw up your life?" Priya is alarmed.

"And Magna Carta doesn't help?" Priya tries.

"Seems not, police bail seems to fall between the cracks." Rita sighs, then brightens, "You know I've seen all four copies now?" she declares.

"Yes, we know." Priya acknowledges, rolling her eyes, and then says, "People like Mohal can really be left with their lives on hold? What about uni? What about the effect on their life?" Priya's outrage on Mohal's behalf continues.

"Yes." Rita goes on, "There's a teacher for example where old accusations were dragged up and the police and CPS just didn't get on with the trial. It was scheduled for December one year and then, because the papers were not ready, the trial was set for the following October! Another 9 months. And the teacher thought he had a complete answer to the case, if they bothered to bring it."

Mohal nods, beginning to see that many people are in a similar predicament to himself.

The door bell at 10 Elm Drive rings. "I'll get it!" Padma yells to the whole house. It is probably the pizza delivery that her offspring have ordered and she is afraid that if Mohal goes to the door to pay he may inadvertently step outside and bring down the wrath of G4S and the police on their family home.

Padma pays the delivery man from 'HappyPizzaCo' who unwraps the pizza from the cocoon of his yellow heat protecting carrier and she takes the pizza through to the pristine kitchen where her children are gathered with Priya. The four sit to set upon the contents of the box, like hyenas with a carcass. Padma fusses round them with plates and cutlery, which they otherwise had no intention of using, and offers soft drinks.Priya and Rita divide a slice of the pizza between them while Nayan and Mohal tuck in appreciatively to the vegetable feast which is set on three different kinds of cheese.

"Wow!" says Priya, "That's a heart stopper!" but she acknowledges the taste is delicious.

"Mmmn!" Mohal cannot speak as his teeth and tongue are glued with cheese, peppers, mushrooms, tomatoes and sweetcorn. When he chews through his mouthful and wipes the grease from his chin he manages.

"At least it's vegetables. Anyway Mr Halliwell had a heart scare and he had a healthy diet... oh!"

"What's up, bruv?" Nayan notices that his brother has stopped eating, his slice poised in the air in front of his mouth.

"Well I've just remembered a strange thing." Mohal says seriously.

Rita cocks her head to one side. "Mmmn? What?"

"When Mr Halliwell had a heart problem he was at Portcullis House so they rushed him across the bridge to Guy's and Thomas's. They kept him on the heart ward for quite a few days. I think they gave him an electric shock or something, to get his heart beating better".

"He was at the hospital where Husna works?" Rita puts in.

Nayan has been included in the secret of who Husna is. Rita and Mohal have yet to tell their parents about the potential witness, they think they will wait until she has signed her statement. Rita thinks this will be a tricky conversation, there is so much she does not understand. She had told Mohal how pretty she thought Husna was and that she liked her, "But I don't get why their religion requires women to be covered up like that." she had added exasperatedly, "It just make them look different." was Rita's verdict. "It's about modesty, isn't it?" Mohal had tried to explain. The Qur'an advises women not to make a display of their beauty in public, to *draw their head coverings over their chests*' is what the Qur'an says, and to '*cast their outer garments over them when outdoors*'".

Rita is mulling over this conversation when she hears

Mohal say,

"Yeah. So anyway, I was at the hospital to see her – to go for a walk in the park – and I'm sure, I'd swear, that there was a bloke at the reception desk, he was behind a lap top but I still saw him."

"And?" Rita presses, (What is the point her brother is trying to make, she wonders?).

"Well he was the same bloke who works as a security guard at Portcullis House!" Mohal takes another bite of pizza at last, while Nayan takes advantage of the hiatus in eating to help himself to another slice.

"You're sure it was the same person? Not just someone like him?" Rita checks.

"Yeah, absolutely. He had short fair hair, sticking up a bit like a punk, know what I mean? And a red mark on his face. I dunno, a birth mark or something. How many people look like that?"

"Do you think it's significant Rita?" Priya asks her friend, taking a sip from her glass of apple juice.

"It could be." says Rita. "It's certainly a coincidence and anything like that needs to be checked out. Sherlock Holmes never liked coincidences." Rita tells her.

"Hang on!" says Nayan finishing the last mouthful of his latest slice of pizza.

"Remember the arrest?" There is no need to explain which arrest Nayan means, the images of Mohal handcuffed on the ground in the middle of a busy London street will be impressed on their memories for a long time.

"What about it?" Priya asks, wiping her mouth as she has finished with the pizza, leaving the rest for the boys.

"I've got it recorded." Nayan says. All three look at him disapprovingly, as if Mohal wants a permanent record of his embarrassment!

"No, listen!" Nayan protests "We should watch the film of it. Because I think there's a security guy in it who fits Mohal's description!"

"Really?" Rita is excited now. "Hurry up and finish the pizza and let's look!"

Chapter

12

"Those who don't know history are destined to repeat it."

Edmund Burke

Wednesday, 30th October 2013 8am

I saw your funeral on TV, Mr Halliwell; perhaps not what you were expecting. Maybe you could see me watching from wherever you are? There weren't many people. There's talk of a memorial service later, but by the time it all comes out at my trial I doubt they will want that. You're probably disappointed, but what do you expect? They may have planned one of those celebrity - filled services - Elton John and George Michael - but I doubt that will be happening, not with the headlines you are going to attract. No one will want to be associated with you when your secret is out.

It's taking the police a long time to put it all together, don't you think? I mean, it's not rocket science. Hello? The room was locked? So suspicion must fall on anyone with a key (you'd think). At this rate the defence will be able to make a laughing stock of the prosecution. They are about as much use as the police investigating that Madeleine McCann case. I wonder about that too, are they really trying? Are they protecting someone? Protecting more than one person perhaps? A ring maybe? Like the circle of rich and powerful surrounding you Mr Halliwell?

They seem short of ideas. They ask the same questions over and over. Where were you between 12 and 2 on Tuesday 23rd? What did you see? What did you hear? What did you do? The questions go on and on til you don't hear them any more.

* * *

Wednesday, 30th October 2013 10am

The Metropolitan Police briefing for Operation Syrinx (which is what the investigation into the death of Mervyn Halliwell has been dubbed by the wisdom of the computer - it is going through a mythology phase) takes place at Scotland Yard at 10am on Wednesday, requiring Inspector Jamie Bridge to make an early start for his drive from Leicester. The grey-haired Detective Superintendent Sharp, who has managed a better night's sleep at last, summarises to a round table of colleagues; these include Deputy Commissioner Alison Tate, who has brown fringe-less hair pulled back into a ponytail, immaculate red lipstick highlighting her mouth, and red finger nails which she sometimes drums on the table. She maintains a watchful scrutiny while also keeping one eye on her phone which she occasionally scrolls through as the DS speaks. A week after the murder, she is there to critique - or 'offer challenge', in the management jargon - the investigation and to suggest lines of inquiry which may have been overlooked and which the defence might exploit. Sergeant Kahn sits opposite Jamie Bridge and is trying to provide moral support for his boss who stands in front of a glass screen on which various pictures and items of information have been placed as the investigation has progressed.

"Tell me again why we let Mohal Patel out on a tag." the Deputy Commissioner says without looking up.

"Two reasons Ma'am." DS Sharp takes the full force of the difficult question. "Firstly, our case against him is mainly circumstantial, and we have not really identified a credible motive, so we need time to build a case the jury will find convincing, find the supporting evidence. There's quite a bit backed up with forensics as well which may tie him to the paint and car scratching incidents. Secondly, as we are searching for a motive we felt that if allowed home Patel may show his hand, may contact someone who's already on our radar; if he feels confident he may slip up."

The DS starts to ruffle his thick grey hair with his hands as he finishes, wishing he had worn a tie to look more formal under the DC's piercing gaze "We covered the flight risk with the passport and the reporting requirement" he adds.

"Mmmn" Alison Tate sounds unconvinced, "On a tag with no access to phones or the internet? Sounds like a tall order for him to contact anyone." she observes.

"We are hoping he will meet up with someone. We have him under surveillance." DS Sharp replies.

"And?" the DC probes.

"The Detective Superintendent sighs," Nothing so far. The stake-out team got excited yesterday when an old Fiesta car drew up outside the family home, but it was only a pizza delivery".

The Deputy Commissioner raises her eyebrows.

"Carry on." she says.

"What have we got?" DS Sharp presses on. "We've got Mohal Patel on CCTV on Westminster Bridge looking shifty. That's just after 2pm on the Tuesday afternoon. The time of death we now know was on that day at 12 or thereabouts. For reasons we can't ascertain, the CCTV in the corridor where the deceased had his office was not working during the relevant time. We cannot be sure what time Mr Halliwell arrived there, although he signed the book at the security desk at 11.50. The MP had his office key in his jacket pocket. We cannot place anyone else in the room other than Mohal Patel, who admits he was there and had evidence on him to prove it." he pauses.

"But, if he did it, why did he hang about? Why wait til 2pm or thereabouts, and then run out of the building?" the DS goes on rhetorically.

"Shame we didn't know about the time of death before we

charged him." interjects the Deputy Commissioner, trying to rewrite history. "Did he panic? Does that explain the delay?" she offers, still scrolling through her phone.

"Possibly. But 2 hours is a long time?" DS Sharp returns.

"A blackout?" Sergeant Kahn suggests.

"Any medical history?" Alison Tate asks. The Sergeant makes a note.

"To build the case we need to know more about Patel's movements that day. And meanwhile there's the so-called alibi witness." DS Sharp looks quizzically at Inspector Bridge as if he is responsible for this inconvenience.

"That may be significant..." Alison Tate again. "She's Muslim? SO15, Counter-Terrorism, are checking out her credentials now. They are looking into any possible extremist connections in the family or among her associates."

"I really don't think..." Jamie Bridge starts to say.

The Deputy Commissioner looks up. "Well what you think doesn't really count at the moment does it?" she says sharply, then, more softly, "I don't think they will find anything either, but we'd look idiots not to check."

Detective Superintendent Sharp tries to get back control of his briefing session, "I agree," he says, "The fact that the witness has come forward, and her fears for her safety, suggest it's all innocent and above board. But it has to be thoroughly checked, Counter-Terrorism got very excited when they first heard about her, it seemed like a lead."

"They should avoid leaping to conclusions." Jamie Bridge fires back, stung by the earlier remark by the Deputy Commissioner, "She sounded genuine on the phone, and really afraid of what might happen if her family find out." he adds.

"Well she hasn't signed the statement yet, it's waiting for her downstairs when she is able to call in. Until then it's all speculative. It may be true, it may not." the DS states.

"Timing is crucial to the case we build." he continues,

pointing to the timeline Sergeant Kahn has contributed to the board. No one argues.

"Mohal Patel says the meeting with Maria Faridi, who we cannot trace by the way, "he says exasperatedly, looking in the direction of the Constable sitting next to Sergeant Khan, who has been charged with identifying this mysterious constituent; so far the emails arranging the meeting have led to a dead end, and there is no other evidence of her on the lap tops of the MP or his secretary. All the Maria Faridis she has contacted have denied being involved.

"Patel says the meeting was for 14.15." he continues, "Miss Matthews says it was 14.15 as well – that was in the diary she printed the day before, but the online version got changed, she does not know how, to 12.15. So either she is lying and she changed it, but I cannot see why, or Mr Halliwell made the change, which he wasn't in the habit of doing, and if he did change it he didn't tell Patel, according to him." The Detective Superintendent pauses for breath while the Constables check their notes and add to them.

"Was the laptop hacked into?" Jamie Bridge asks, adding, "Mohal Patel's solicitor has put that forward as a theory." as he intercepts another exchange of annoyed looks between the Superintendent and the Deputy Commissioner.

"It's possible, the tech boys say, they are still running some checks but there is some suspicious software on there." the DS concedes.

"If not Mohal Patel, then who?" Alison Tate asks. "What about the deceased's associates?"

Sergeant Kahn answers to give his boss some relief, "Well the wife is devastated. Genuine grief, largely over losing the chance to be Lady Halliwell, in my opinion, and losing out on Conservative Party dinners."

"Oh dear." the DC responds, not sounding sympathetic "No children?"

The Sergeant confirms, "No, none. There's a younger

brother with a wife and a disabled child. Mr Halliwell lent him money and looking into the family history, the MP was actually adopted by the brother's father..."

"Sounds interesting." the DC interrupts, "Anything worth pursuing there? Families fall out over money, and the history sounds complicated too."

Sergeant Kahn gestures to the Constable to contribute while he helps himself to a glass of water from the jug in the middle of the table.

"As regards the history Ma'am" the Constable starts, "We looked at the MP's birth certificate. Turns out he was illegitimate. Not a big deal these days but more of a stigma forty odd years ago, and his mother was only 15 at the time. Something you never heard about during his life, he kept that fact a secret. His mother died several years ago".

"But he was adopted?" the DC tries to move the story along.

"Yes." the Constable continues, "His mother married when she was 20 and the husband, the father of her second son, Martin, adopted Mervyn."

"So they all grew up together as one happy family." the Sergeant adds.

"We are sure about that? No jealousy or resentment? After all the MP was very successful, always in the public eye, and the brother..?" she makes the sentence into a question by raising the tone of her voice.

"He runs a gardening business. He cuts lawns, mends walls, paints fences and puts in water features, that sort of thing. I have his card." the Constable says as if she can put the officers in touch if they need some gardening work doing.

"Tell me about the loan." the DC persists.

"Mr Halliwell lent his brother money to adapt his house for his disabled son, he's confined to a wheelchair. They put in a wet room." the Sergeant says.

"Yes, yes, spare me the makeover details." the Deputy

Commissioner scrolls more furiously on her phone as she interrupts.

"We haven't found any sign that the relationship was less than amicable, Ma'am. The brother was paying off the loan." Sergeant Kahn clarifies.

"Hmmn, so he's unlikely to have wanted the MP dead? To have arranged for someone to do it? We need to look at all the angles." she retorts.

"That's right." the DS resumes, "We do and we are. The brother looks clean."

"What about his staff?" the Deputy Commissioner continues the inquisition.

The DS says, "The Secretary, Camilla Matthews, dated various MPs in the past – it's quite common for secretaries and MPs to have relationships apparently; is anyone old enough to remember Cecil Parkinson?" he asks looking round the table but there are no flickers of recognition at the name so he continues, "But there's no suggestion that she had a liaison with Mr Halliwell, although she was clearly fond of him, in a maternal kind of way. She is going to be lost without her role."

"And her laptop." adds Sergeant Kahn (Camilla has been on the phone again that morning checking when hers will be returned). "But there's no sign of any rift between them, nothing to suggest she might wish him harm."

"Unless she made advances and was rebuffed?" the DC suggests, "And check there's nothing behind this persistence over the computer."

The Constables make more notes.

"Sebastian Stainer, the political adviser, had been with Halliwell for about 3 months." the Detective Superintendent continues. "He had previously worked with another Minister. He just talks politics, focus groups and whether issues 'cut through' with voters whatever that means. It's hard to engage with him in proper English. To be honest he's so far off the planet I cannot see he would be likely to commit so basic a crime, something so real and physical."

The Deputy Commissioner sits back in her chair, putting down her phone for a moment. "Anyone else?" she says, "Other interns?"

The Sergeant explains, "They do a few weeks or months, then move on, mostly back to university. Some stay longer than others. Sometimes there's more than one."

"So no one left unexpectedly?" the DC checks.

"Not that we can find out, but it would be hard to tell. No one keeps proper records as they are not employed..." the DS explains, "DI Harris is looking into the political angles but that's not producing anything .When they say MPs cross swords they don't mean literally!" he goes on.

"Harris had a pretty frosty exchange with the Permanent Secretary at the Department I gather," Detective Superintendent Sharp continues, "He did a sort of Sir Humphrey – you know from Yes Minister - managed to offer full cooperation while putting so many obstacles in our way it was practically impossible. But the officials don't seem to have been around Portcullis House much, and not on the day in question, and there's nothing suspicious about any of the ones who worked most closely with the MP."

"Private life then, these internet rumours?" says the DC gesturing to the Constable to pour her a glass of the water.

"We are looking into it of course." the Sergeant puts in, looking at his boss rather than the Deputy Commissioner, "We are capturing details of the solid allegations and there is also a lot of vague innuendo. He does seem to have attracted some nasty trolls though. Homophobic mostly but a few making hints of a wilder side to the MP."

"He was gay then?" the Deputy Commissioner clarifies.

The DS shrugs his shoulders equivocally.

Sergeant Kahn intervenes. "His London flat was very anonymous could have been a hotel room, no picture of the lady wife in there. The Oakham House was like a branch of Laura Ashley, lots of evidence of the wife's touch everywhere. There was a wedding picture and one of Halliwell with his brother and the disabled nephew."

"So maybe he was bisexual?" the Constable suggests.

"It's not uncommon. We haven't unearthed any long term same sex relationships, only allegations of one night stands, and some inappropriate behaviour, misreading signals, that sort of thing." the Sergeant explains.

"He wouldn't be the first public figure to suppress his sexuality." adds Detective Superintendent Sharp, "Which is daft. It just exposes you to the risk of blackmail, but there's no evidence that he was being blackmailed."he adds hastily before Alison Tate can ask," And we're getting off the point."

"There are no suspicious names in the visitors' book that day or any day around then." the Detective Superintendent goes on.

"Someone with a grudge?" offers Sergeant Kahn, still thinking of the unsavoury rumours appearing on social network sites.

"Someone with a knife." Deputy Commissioner Tate says pointedly. "Amateur or professional?" she asks.

"Hard to tell," concedes DS Sharp, "Probably male in view of the strength needed, the knife penetrated a long way." then he adds, "Someone he knew or trusted, he was sitting down and there are no defence wounds."

"Or someone who came into the room and took him by surprise." the DC offers. Then, "Does Patel have combat training?" is the Deputy Commissioner's next question.

"Not exactly." Sergeant Kahn tells her, "He was in the cadet force at school for a few weeks but soon left. His school report says he wasn't the outdoor type and he wasn't really interested in the physical effort involved."

"Any history of violence?" Alison Tate checks.

"We have never had any trouble with the family." Jamie

Bridge feels he should intervene. "Mohal has been stopped in his car a few times but we never charged him with anything, not so much as a caution." he tells the meeting.

"He has a temper." Sergeant Kahn contributes, "He's lost his rag with police officers doing stop and search, and we've seen him get angry in the interview room." he looks to his boss for support, the DS nods, "so the CPS barrister could probably get him to do it in to dock." he adds.

"Mmmn." Alison Tate sips her water, leaving a crimson imprint on the rim of her glass. "What have we got on motive?" she queries.

"Halliwell's stance on Syria. His opposition to people going there to fight, or to support charities there. Patel has signed petitions and been to university campus meetings about it".

"Why Halliwell?" the DC asks next.

"Proximity." DS Sharp returns. "Patel got to work with him because he's a Leicester MP and takes interns. He may have realised then what the MP's views were or he may have learnt about them when they were working together." he rehearses the arguments.

"And why that day?" Alison Tate persists before Jamie Bridge can protest again about Mohal's character.

"Opportunity. He may have planned it for weeks, then saw his chance." DS Sharp answers.

"How did he get a knife into the building?" the DC wants to know.

Sergeant Kahn supplies, "The security guards were a bit sheepish. They admit they are not as strict with the staff as with the visitors. They figure they have been security vetted to get their passes .So he could have slipped it past them."

"If he planned it, why not plan what to do with the knife afterwards? Throwing it in the river looks spontaneous. Have we checked whether it's washed up at all?" the DC carries on.

Before the DS can answer, a mobile phone rings out

and Jamie Bridge realises it is his. The Superintendent and Deputy Commissioner look sharply at him as he fumbles to take the phone from his pocket. Inspector Bridge sees the call is from Rita. "I'll have to take this." he says as he stands (scarcely believing he is saying this in front of so senior a gathering). Inspector Bridge walks out of the room.

"Hello Rita. Sorry, I was in a meeting. How can I help you?" he says when he reaches the corridor.

"Mohal may have remembered something important." Rita tells him. She is calling from school in a study period and cannot talk for long "A man. He saw him at the hospital – Guy's and Thomas's - and he saw him on security duty at Portcullis House. It may be nothing but…"

"Okay Rita. It may be a guard who works in both places but I'll talk to the guys here." ('Guys? Is he calling Scotland Yard's senior officers guys?' Jamie Bridge thinks to himself) "and get back to you. We have photos of the security people so Mohal may be able to identify the man from those. Give me 30 minutes and I'll call you back."

"I'll have to ring you at lunchtime." Rita replies. "We are not supposed to take calls during lessons".

Jamie Bridge strides back into the briefing, absent-mindedly patting his phone against his lips. The gesture serves to hide the grin of satisfaction on his face that he has a new line of inquiry for the briefing to consider.

Chapter

13

"I desire not to keep my place in this government an hour longer than I may preserve England in its just rights, and may protect this people of God in such a just liberty of their consciences."
> Oliver Cromwell's speech dissolving the First Protectorate Parliament, 22nd January 1655.

Wednesday, 30th October 2013 4pm

By the middle of the afternoon, Jamie Bridge has sped northwards to Leicester to assist with the interview of Mohal Patel at Leicester police station. His Sergeant has arranged for the Met to email over photographs of all the security staff at Portcullis House and he has these assembled on a laptop, together with some random other faces, so that Mohal can point out the person, if he recognises him, in an identity parade. The Deputy Commissioner and DS Sharp had been sceptical when Jamie had explained Rita's new information to the briefing. But they conceded the evidence might be relevant and should be pursued; Sergeant Kahn was asked to keep the CPS informed in case there was a change of tack.

The Inspector arrives to find Mohal in an interview room with Tim Beresford and Sergeant Griffiths, one of the officers who had searched Rita's house. Rita had wanted to attend the interview but was overruled by her parents ("You have done enough. You need to concentrate on your school work. This is an important year for you.").

"Now Mr Patel." Jamie Bridge says after introductions have been made. "You have information that may help us? You want to make a statement?" he asks across the chipped wooden veneer surface of the MDF table at which they are sitting, facing each other.

"Yes" Mohal leans forward, "I remembered a guy."

"Okay, let's take this a bit at a time." Jamie Bridge advises, and Mohal tells his story; how Mr Halliwell was rushed to hospital in September (Inspector Bridge checks his notes, the Metroplitan Police have this information on their timeline, Miss Matthews had mentioned it; the MP was in hospital for 4 days towards the end of September); Mohal goes on to explain how this was Guy's and Thomas's hospital where – Mohal hesitates and looks at Mr Beresford who assists, "Where an acquaintance of Mr Patel works and whom he was visiting. This is the same person who has provided a statement as to Mr Patel's whereabouts on the day of the murder. The identity is to remain undisclosed in the statement." Tim Beresford states. All in the room are aware that Husna had called at Scotland Yard that lunchtime and signed the statement she gave to Jamie Bridge. The Metropolitan Police are digesting this and have yet to react.

The Inspector nods his understanding and encourages Mohal to continue,

"So I went to the reception desk and I caught sight of a bloke, he was crouching behind a laptop, I got the impression he was hoping to hide from me. I didn't think about it at the time, but now I wonder – it was one of the security guards at Portcullis House."

"One of the guards on duty on the day of the murder?" the Sergeant asks.

"I don't know… except that we saw him, if you look at the video of my arrest - he's on the film, running towards me with the police officer with the gun – so he probably was on duty." Mohal offers.

"Mmmn" says Jamie Bridge non-commitally. This story, as DS Sharp and Deputy Commissioner Tate were keen to emphasise in London, is rather convenient, as is his alibi witness, and, like everything else Mohal has said about the events, there is only his word for it. The fact that there is a man on the film of his arrest who he is now alleging was at the hospital when Mervyn Halliwell was there is less, rather than more, helpful, to Mohal the Superintendent thought – Mohal could have seen the film and decided to make up the story about the hospital, he had considered, sceptically.

"See if you can see him." The Sergeant takes Mohal through photographs compiled on a laptop, one by one, not disclosing which are of security staff and which are of men not connected with the inquiry, in case Mohal is just using the opportunity to throw suspicion elsewhere.

Mohal shakes his head several times, then "Yes! That's him. There's the spiky hair and the mark on his face!" he says excitedly.

Inspector and Sergeant peer at the picture of a blond man, in his twenties, with a disctinctive red birth mark across his face in the shape of an inverted question mark which twists from his right eye across his cheek and rests against his sharp-shaped nose. They are both thinking, this individual stands out and if involved in the murder of Mervyn Halliwell was very daring indeed.

"Okay Mr Patel. You can go now. We will look into this." Jamie Bridge tells Mohal. The Sergeant leaves with the laptop to check with Sergeant Kahn at Scotland Yard what is known about the identified individual. Mohal rises quickly, glad to leave but anxious too. Will this help clear his name?

"And there's no question of looking at CCTV evidence of the route which Mr Patel took with, with his acquaintance?" Mr Beresford rises too but is not yet ready to leave.

"We can't justify that. It would be like looking for a needle in a haystack. The defence can go through it all if you want." Jamie Bridge trots out the official line.

"Mmmn. That's what I thought." Mr Beresford says, "May be worth us paying to look at the station cameras at least. If we can show Mohal was there at 12 you would have to drop the case now the time of death has been established as at that time…"

"Oh!" Mohal suddenly exclaims, clasping his hands to his head as if in pain and sitting down again. Mr Beresford and the Inspector look startled and sit down too.

"What is it?" Jamie Bridge asks. "Are you unwell? Do you want a doctor?" he offers, concerned.

"No, no, I just remembered something else. When we were at Victoria Station there was a promotion going on – for chocolate." Mohal says hurriedly.

Inspector and Solicitor exchange puzzled looks, what has this to do with anything? Free chocolate will not provide an alibi.

"They were filming. Well people on the station were shown on a big screen. People were dancing and waving. The theme was 'HAPPINESS' I recall. The chocolate people wanted to know what makes you happy. At first we didn't realise we were on the screen – we would have avoided it if we could – but then we got caught up in the whole thing, the sales people were very enthusiastic. We joined in a dance, a conga around the station, in front of the platforms, we could see ourselves on the big screen. Do you think they will have kept the film? Or if anyone would remember us?" he asks hopefully.

Jamie Bridge and Tim Beresford make more notes; Mr Beresford says he will get someone to check with the chocolate company. Mohal and his lawyer finally leave the room. The Inspector shakes his head. 'Can it be chocolate that saves Mohal Patel?' he thinks.

Chapter

14

"Boys do now cry 'Kiss my Parliament!' instead of 'Kiss my arse!' so great and general a contempt is the Rump come to among all men, good and bad."

Samuel Pepys on the Parliament
which persisted under
Richard Cromwell before
the restoration of Charles II

Thursday, October 31st 2013 5pm

Hallowe'en. Ghosts and ghouls, witches and warlocks stalk the streets. Pumpkin lanterns adorn windows and the emphasis is on spooks and scary things. Trick or treat? It doesn't get scarier than that! Don't go to strangers' houses. ("Hats off Strangers" the Police Inspector says at the State Opening of Parliament when the Speaker's procession approaches the Central Lobby, the Speaker in breeches and waistcoat and his train held up by a page, and the police officers take off their helmets. That's pretty spooky if you ask me!)

They believe the man and his denials! They promote him! They give him a Ministerial post. They put him on a select committee that looks at people going to Syria. They are going to need a big carpet to sweep under when I've finished telling the truth about what is going on!

My life went on hold after he did that to me. I realised I couldn't protect myself. I couldn't trust anyone. I lived on automatic pilot. I slept on the streets. It was when I was sleeping rough, by a gym, that I got my lucky break. They needed a cleaner. So I took the job. Long hours and minimum wage but I learnt about zero-hours contracts; how to get taken on as a waiter, a hospital porter or a security guard for example. I met two guys who were personal trainers and they showed me round the gym. So I took to exercise and built myself up. I learnt martial arts and self defence. It made me feel more secure. It made me feel powerful.

* * *

Thursday, October 31st 2013 6pm

Tim Beresford calls a meeting to review where they are. All day he has been talking to officers at Scotland Yard, and Inspector Bridge of the Leicester police, trying to input the evidence which is gathering and to understand what is happening with the investigation.

Husna's statement as to Mohal's movements, together with the time of death as 12 o'clock, and the film from the chocolate company, seem to him to put Mohal completely in the clear, but the police and CPS are slow to digest and accept this, especially as they have yet to apprehend another suspect. Mr Beresford knows from experience that having leapt too quickly to the conclusion that Mohal was guilty they will move cautiously before letting him go and arresting anyone else.

Mr Beresford had left a message with the marketing department of the chocolate manufacturers as soon as he and Mohal had left the Leicester police station the day before. He was afraid they would have destroyed the film but the marketing manager had called back first thing in the morning and was very helpful.

"Of course!" she had said "Our theme is Happiness. How can we not contribute to this young man's happiness? Let us know if we can use the story at some point." and she arranged for the film from Victoria Station on that day to be uploaded and emailed to the police and to Tim Beresford.

He and his assistant had scanned the footage anxiously. There was Victoria Station, there was a conga line of passengers, tourists, visitors, some in wheelchairs, laughing and shouting, waving at the screen when they saw themselves and there – there was Mohal Patel and a young lady in a long skirt and a headscarf, laughing as if they had no cares in the world and no breath left. Tim Beresford had breathed a satisfied sigh. The time in the corner of the film said 12.01pm.

"So we have the film which puts you clearly well away from Portcullis House at the time of the murder." Mr Beresford tells Mohal, "And there is more we can investigate now we have …er… the statement of your acquaintance." He looks concernedly round the table. Padma is at home with Nayan ("You can't neglect your homework.") but Jahi is at the meeting, as is Rita. Mohal had explained to his parents about Husna when he returned from the police station, on Wednesday evening, when it was clear she had signed her statement. They had heard his news in silence. Relieved and grateful that a stranger was able to help their son, puzzled and worried that the person in question is a Muslim girl. Jahi had wanted to ask a lot of questions, such as how could his son spend time with a girl of that religion? But Padma had raised her hand to stop him, a gesture she used in their marriage rarely but effectively. It meant "Let us discuss this among ourselves. Do not leap into a discussion in front of the children." So their response had been muted and, even when they came to discuss the issue alone together later, they had resolved to say as little as possible until Mohal's name could be cleared; that was the priority they agreed.

Tim Beresford goes on, "From the statement, it looks to me that it may be worthwhile exploring,

the CCTV at the Boots store where you bought the sandwiches

the vendors in the park on the route you took, they have sharp eyes and may have noticed you go by; the difficulty there is being sure of the particular day but there may be other factors which help with that. Mobile phone records for-"

Mr Beresford's list is interrupted by his own mobile phone ringing. "One moment," he says to the meeting and stands to listen to the caller. It is Detective Superintendent Sharp from the Metropolitan Police. "I may have some better news for you." he says.

Chapter

15

"Ninety per cent of the politicians give the other ten per cent a bad name."

Henry A Kissinger

Friday, 1st November 2013 1pm

I think they've worked it out. Even the police aren't so stupid. I wonder if they have enough evidence, though. Circumstantial is one thing – right place (wrong place?) right time –but unless I confess (shall I?) I don't see why I should make it easy for them. Without the knife and any CCTV for the corridor at the time, they'll struggle. There'll be no DNA, I was careful about that, and no finger prints (especially after that stupid boy – how fortuitous- trampled over the scene and spread Halliwell's blood about. Thanks Mohal, I owe you!).

As a security guard I watched Halliwell come and go, even got to frisk him sometimes, imagine being so close! I swapped shifts to keep an eye on him while I made my plans. I got the knife into the building easily enough, old Charlie never checks the guards' bags properly. I just kept it in my locker until I needed it. I disabled the CCTV on the corridor for a couple of hours. I waited until Halliwell was sitting in the room, stabbed him and locked the door with my pass key. I kept the knife and threw it down a drain while all the attention was on that idiot getting himself arrested in public. I made out I was looking for evidence when I was actually disposing of it!

I would have done it earlier, but when Halliwell got ill I thought maybe I could finish him off in hospital. Something poetic about that? So I took the zero hours porter work and found my way about. It wasn't easy, there are too many signs with long words, I do not know how patients find the right ward or clinic. Why do they not use pictures? A drawing of a heart for the heart ward (cardiology they insist on calling it), where Halliwell was for example; you could have pictures of babies for maternity, old people for geriatric wards and children for paediatric wards; what would the cancer (oncology) sign be? Maybe a red lightning bolt, that's how I think of it.

I got onto the floor where they were treating him, the heart ward, but there were too many people around for me to make a move – a constant procession in and out of his room of medics, cleaners, catering staff, his own staff – that spoilt toff Sebastian Stainer and that fat secretary, Camilla Matthews. I watched from a distance so they never realised I was there. But they never left him in peace! No wonder he had a heart problem! I nearly had a heart attack myself when I saw that stupid boy in reception at the hospital. I had to think quickly in case he recognised me. I dodged behind a computer, I don't think he saw me.

When they come, how will it be? Will there be a knock on the door, a ring on the bell? A shout like on TV – "armed police, come out with your arms in the air", make me lie on the ground while they check I don't have a gun? Train a gun on me, that tell-tale red light like in that film with Al Pacino? Perhaps they'll have a tazer with them. They seem pretty keen to use them these days, the sadists. Well I don't want to be in pain and I do want to be in full control of myself so I won't give them the chance or the satisfaction.

Do I tell them why I did it, though? Or shall I save it for my trial? I shall use my day in court to expose Halliwell! Then watch the complaints come crawling out of the woodwork. All those people who suffered like I did will finally be listened to – too late! Should I have killed him? Was it a bit harsh? No, I don't think so. Also death was too good. I should have made him suffer. I should at least have made sure he understood. Did he get it? Hard to say. What do we think about when know we are going to die? Regrets? Pain? Hope it won't happen? I wasn't looking at his face but he may have seen mine in the mirror. I don't know if he recognised me. Doubt it.

I was nothing to him. He used me and forgot about me. Like a wrapper you throw away. No I don't think he really got his comeuppance. But that's not important to me. Someone had to act. And I did.I expect I'll be well treated in prison. MPs can't be popular and I can handle myself with mens attention now. I'll find someone to be nice to me and use them for protection. I'll be okay. I wonder if I will come out a drug addict? They say drugs are more easily available inside than outside. So it's possible. I'm not bothered. If Her Majesty's pleasure makes me a junkie then Her Majesty's Government will just have to support me when I get out. I can't be expected to work if I'm high on drugs, can I? I'll get the medics to sign me off – depression, mental health, that sort of thing, who cares. I'll have time inside to research the rules and how to fake the symptoms. That's one thing, unless those feather-bedded whingers in Parliament change their minds, I won't be voting for them for a while, not when I'm inside, even though the Human Rights Court thinks prisoners should be able to vote. Well none of them is worth voting for anyway.

I've watched them close up, remember, at their cocktail parties and coming and going at PCH and what a bunch! The men overfed like corn fed chicken, the women not eating enough so they look ok on the TV, giving themselves scary chicken necks and bulging eyes. There were a few decent ones, I'll give you that. The odd one who acknowledged me, even sympathised with my working hours and conditions, tried to be no trouble. But they were the exception. That's why they stood out. Pools of humanity in the sludge pit. Bullies full of their own opinions, trapped by their parties into repeating lines (lies?) to take and pre-prepared mantras - 'hard working families' 'squeezed middle' 'cost of living crisis' 'Big Society'. It's as if they think people have such a small attention span, two or three word slogans are all the great British public can grasp apparently. They all look the same, dress the same, act the same. You can't tell who's in which party in the main. And the policies get more similar. I guess I've just been too close to them, seen things people shouldn't see, what is that saying about sausages and sausage factories?

But how ever pompous and ridiculous and self satisfied they are they have no right to take advantage of young people, of innocent people, of people who trust them, of people who are attracted to them because of their powerful personalities. They have no right to abuse their position, to use people to do things they don't want to do, Those parties, the drinks were flowing, there were drugs around if you wanted them, 5 star hotels,houses with pools, it would make anyone's head swim and at the end of all that there is the dark, the dirty deeds, the price you pay for being enticed and seduced and caught in the spider's web and when you're there it's sticky and it's tricky and you can't escape,you have to find a way and I found a way...

Oh, there's a knock on the door.

"Mr James?"

"Mr James, it's the police".

"Will you let us in Mr James?"

Are they standing at my door with one of those battering rams? Will they knock the door down if I don't answer?

Oh well I'd better let them in.

Chapter

16

"The only thing necessary for the triumph of evil is for good men to do nothing."

Edmund Burke

Saturday, 2nd November 2013 11am

On Saturday morning Mr Patel (no relation), drawing up outside Rita's house in his red Corsa, is greeted with a strange sight. Parked outside the house is a black Ford Focus he does not recognise and a man in black trousers and t-shirt is just climbing into it and about to leave. Meanwhile, behind him, Mohal Patel emerges through the front door, a garland of flowers round his neck, and does a sort of dance, the kind footballers do when celebrating goals. He dances down the driveway and onto the pavement,he dances along the pavement,he waves to the house,he crosses the street and comes back again, more running than dancing now, his arms splayed out as if he is pretending to be an aeroplane.

Mohal's younger brother appears (not garlanded) and joins in this strange ritual. Now they look like they are pretending to be First World War fighter pilots in a dogfight, or imitating the Red Arrows display team. They swoop and dive towards one another, then swerve away, laughing, and they make pretend goggles with their hands over their eyes. Rita's parents appear next, standing on the doorstep, hugging each other and grinning at their sons.

'What can be happening?' Mr Patel wonders. 'Is it Mohal's birthday perhaps?' Finally, his pupil squeezes past her mother and father who are in the doorway and walks to the car as if nothing strange is happening at all.

"Do I detect a smile Miss Patel?" Mr Patel tries as Rita composes herself and checks her mirrors and seat position.

"Something to celebrate in your family?" he probes further.

"Sort of." Rita nods.

The Detective Superintendent from the Metropolitan Police had followed up his call to Mr Beresford and confirmed on Friday evening that they had another suspect in custody and that the charges against Mohal were being dropped. Scotland Yard would not confirm the suspect was the security guard identified by Mohal, but Inspector Bridge was prepared to admit this was the case to Tim Beresford, off the record.

The confirmation had come too late for G4S to be sent to Elm Drive on Friday night, so Mohal spent one more night with his tag on his leg and it was Saturday morning before their operative arrived to release him and take away the equipment that had been lurking ominously on the bookcase in the living room. It was the culmination of this scene that Mr Patel had witnessed. As soon as his incarceration was over Mohal had wanted to run and run outside, just to prove he was free and Rita, to celebrate, had decorated him with a garland she had managed to acquire the day before.

Everyone in the house was so relieved. Padma had wept tears of joy when Scotland Yard had told Mohal the news and immediately got on the phone to her sister, Jaina. "Now we can celebrate Diwali all together!" Jaina had said. Her children, twin girls slightly younger than Nayan, had been getting excited and attending aspects of the 5 day festival which had started at the beginning of the month. Things had looked too dark then for Bandhu and Jaina to invite their relatives to join them in celebrating. Now everything had changed and they could join the 35,000 or so people who were expected to take part. They could go together in traditional dress, walk along the golden mile on Belgrave Road and attend the parades and fireworks in the City, the largest Diwali celebrations outside India. The sisters made arrangements to meet the next day by the statue of Mahatma Gandhi.

Jahi had telephoned Aunty Gee and his relatives in India to tell them the good news and Rita had skyped Priya.

Priya was elated. "I knew it would be all right!" she said, "Mohal must be so happy!" Then she added "They could not possibly have gone ahead and tried him! It just wouldn't have been fair and isn't your Magna Whatsit about justice and fairness?"

"It's not my Magna Carta." Rita pointed out, "But yeah, to no man – than includes women – will we deny or delay justice."

Mohal, thinking it would be all right, had texted Husna the previous evening, when they got the news, and thanked her for her help.

"Can we have the Xbox back now?" Nayan asked, pleased to see his older brother's spirits restored and the family tension broken. He had found it hard at school, explaining that their India holiday had been cut short but not able to say why to his friends, and finding it difficult to concentrate on his lessons as he feared that more bad news might await when he got home.

"I hope I get my computer back soon." says Jahi to his wife, "I must catch up with the practice accounts. And what about my white paint?"

Rita knows her mother is planning a celebratory meal for them all that evening. "I'll eat mine in the garden." says Mohal, "Even if it's raining! I don't ever want to feel like I'm stuck indoors again."

"I'm pleased to hear it." says Jahi, hoping it means his oldest child will spend less time on the sofa in future.

All this happiness Rita keeps to herself, although it lights up her eyes and dances across her lips, as she drives away from the kerb.

Rita Patel returns in
Body in Space

ISBN: 978-1-910779-68-2

ISBN: 978-1-910779-69-9

ISBN: 978-1-910779-70-5

ISBN: 978-1-910779-71-2

ISBN: 978-1-910779-72-9

ISBN: 978-1-910779-73-6

ISBN: 978-1-910779-74-3

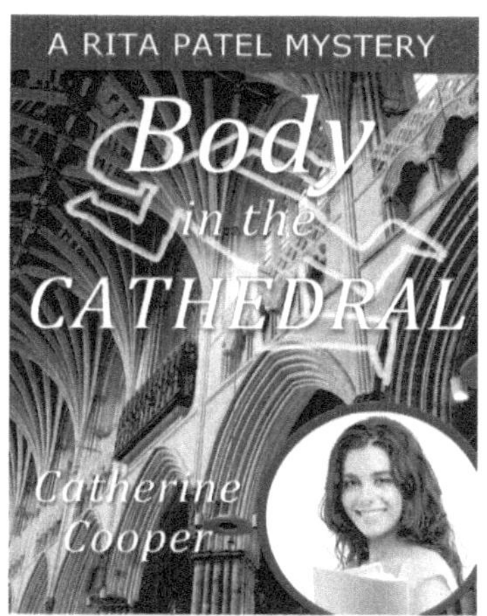

ISBN: 978-1-910779-75-0